The perfe

Suddenly, Elizabeth understood why people loved to act. Something magic was happening to her. She didn't feel embarrassed to be auditioning opposite Todd now, because she wasn't Elizabeth anymore. She wasn't Jessica either. She was Juliet.

She took a step forward and held out both arms, as if to embrace the night. "Romeo, doff thy name; / And for that name, which is no part of thee, / Take all myself."

"Bravo!" *Mr. Bowman yelled. He shot out of his seat and began hurrying up the stage steps.*

All around her, people were applauding and whistling.

"Look," *she heard Todd say as he showed his arm to Denny Jacobson.* "I've got goose bumps."

Elizabeth had never felt such a rush of joy and pride. Everywhere she looked, she saw faces beaming with admiration and enthusiasm.

She couldn't believe it. She had made the role her own. She had found a bit of Juliet in plain old Elizabeth Wakefield.

"Great job, Jessica," *Mr. Bowman said warmly.*

Jessica?

Elizabeth's heart began to sink slowly into her stomach.

SWEET VALLEY TWINS

Romeo and 2 Juliets

Written by
Jamie Suzanne

Created by
FRANCINE PASCAL

BANTAM BOOKS
NEW YORK · TORONTO · LONDON · SYDNEY · AUCKLAND

RL 4, 008-012

ROMEO AND 2 JULIETS
A Bantam Book / January 1995

Sweet Valley High® *and Sweet Valley Twins*™ *are*
registered trademarks of Francine Pascal

Conceived by Francine Pascal

Produced by Daniel Weiss Associates, Inc.
33 West 17th Street
New York, NY 10011

Cover art by James Mathewuse

ISBN: 0-553-48105-3

Published simultaneously in the United States and Canada

Bantam Books are published by Bantam Books, a division of Bantam
Doubleday Dell Publishing Group, Inc. Its trademark, consisting of the
words "Bantam Books" and the portrayal of a rooster, is registered in the
U.S. Patent and Trademark Office and in other countries. Marca
Registrada. Bantam Books, 1540 Broadway, New York, New York 10036.

PRINTED IN THE UNITED STATES OF AMERICA

OPM   0 9 8 7 6 5 4 3 2 1

To Bradley Scott Halpern

One

"Ahhhh-chooo! Excuse be," Leslie Forsythe said, sniffling. Jessica Wakefield giggled. She was sitting in her English class on Monday morning, and so many people at Sweet Valley Middle School had come down with the flu or a cold recently that it was becoming a joke.

"Gesundheit," Mr. Bowman said as he looked around the room at all the empty seats. "I want everybody who's still here to make an effort to stay healthy," he said. "We're about to begin a very interesting project, and you won't want to miss it."

Jessica sighed as she watched Mr. Bowman lift a thick stack of papers from his desk. Mr. Bowman was OK for a teacher, but Jessica thought English was a pretty boring subject. She didn't like the looks of all that paper.

"Take one copy and pass the rest down," Mr. Bowman instructed as he handed a stack to Dennis Cookman, who was sitting at the head of his row.

Jessica examined her copy once Lila Fowler passed her the stack. The words *Romeo and Juliet* were typed on the front page. Jessica felt a flicker of happy surprise. She had heard about *Romeo and Juliet* all her life. She had never actually read it or seen the movie, but she knew it was about love and that it had some teenagers in it.

"*Two households, both alike in dignity, | In fair Verona, where we lay our scene, | From ancient grudge break to new mutiny,*" Dennis Cookman read out loud in a high, silly voice. "What's *that* supposed to mean? What's with all those dumb fancy words? This stuff is for girls." He tried to thrust his copy at Amy Sutton.

Blushing, Amy tried to thrust it back. "Not this girl."

Somewhere in the back row, one of the boys began making kissing noises.

Mr. Bowman cleared his throat and rapped on the edge of his desk. "Shakespeare is for everybody," he corrected. "And whoever is making that noise, stop it."

"Shakespeare's a total bore," Ken Matthews grumbled. "He hasn't written anything new in four hundred years."

"Well, that's true," Mr. Bowman said. "He is dead, after all. But his work is timeless and very often relevant to modern life. Which plays do you find so boring?"

Ken shifted uncomfortably in his chair. "Well . . . uh . . . I haven't exactly read any Shakespeare plays. But I know what they're like, and I wouldn't be into them."

"Me neither," Dennis Cookman said.

Mr. Bowman smiled slightly. "Has *anyone* in the class ever seen or read a Shakespeare play?"

There were a lot of murmured no's.

As Jessica cast her eyes over the play, she could see why no one had ever read Shakespeare. *I thought this was supposed to be romantic,* she said to herself. She didn't see anything about going out on dates or kissing. All she saw were long and boring chunks of poetry. And it didn't even rhyme.

She looked around the room. Near the front, her sister, Elizabeth, was earnestly poring over the script on her desk. *Figures,* Jessica thought. *Leave it to Elizabeth to get excited about this boring stuff.*

Jessica and Elizabeth Wakefield were identical twins. Both girls were twelve years old and sixth-graders at Sweet Valley Middle School in Sweet Valley, California. They had the same long, sun-streaked blond hair, the same blue-green eyes, and the same dimple in their left cheeks.

But inside, the girls were as different as night and day. Elizabeth was the more serious twin. She was really into reading and writing. In fact, she was the editor-in-chief of the *Sixers,* the official sixth-grade newspaper of Sweet Valley Middle School. Elizabeth's best friends, Amy Sutton and Maria Slater, were serious and practical, too. Jessica thought they were boring.

Jessica was more into glamour. She was a member of the exclusive Unicorn Club, which was made up of the prettiest and most popular girls at Sweet Valley Middle School. She loved to read articles about movie stars and models and wanted to be glamorous and famous when she grew up.

Jessica sighed again as she turned the page.

"Jessica?" Mr. Bowman said. "Did you have something to say?"

Normally, Jessica didn't like to be called on in class—teachers always seemed to single her out when she didn't have an answer ready. But today she knew what she wanted to say, and she felt confident that the class shared her opinion. "This stuff is too hard to read," she said.

Mr. Bowman nodded. "Yes, a Shakespeare play is hard to read—which is why we're not going to read it."

Jessica looked at him hopefully. "We're not?"

"No, we're not. We're going to *act* it."

"Act it?" Lila Fowler repeated.

"Act it," Mr. Bowman confirmed.

Act it! Jessica thought as the whole room began to buzz with excitement. Reading something boring was boring. But acting it was different. Acting was totally glamorous. Jessica squirmed in her seat as she thought about the makeup and the costumes and the spotlight.

"Cool," Randy Mason commented. "Check out the sword fight on page two."

"How many guys?" Aaron Dallas asked.

"Quiet, please," Mr. Bowman said. "Before you start counting parts, you should know that we're not going to do the whole play. We're going to do a mini-production. The highlights of the play. The major scenes and speeches."

"When will the performance be?" Melissa McCormick asked.

"We'll be performing a week from Friday," Mr. Bowman answered. "Which means we won't have a lot of time for all the formalities—dress rehearsals, technical rehearsals, et cetera. We're going to have to put this together in a very short amount of time. But we will try to make the occasion as gala as possible. Our mini-production will take place at night, and I hope you will all invite your parents and siblings."

"Will we wear costumes?" Lila Fowler asked, twirling a strand of her long brown hair.

Mr. Bowman nodded. "Yes, we will. The drama coach at Sweet Valley High has donated some costumes from a production they did several months ago. And we'll even have special effects—like padding and fake warts."

"Warts!" Lila said, making a face. "What are warts doing in a romantic play like *Romeo and Juliet?*"

"The warts are for whoever plays Juliet's old, fat nurse," Mr. Bowman said, smiling. "And I must say, these warts are absolutely hideous. They should add a lot of atmosphere to the play."

Jessica shivered. She felt sorry for whoever would have to play Juliet's nurse.

"We'll have props, too," Mr. Bowman continued. "We'll have swords and—"

"All right!" Ken Matthews broke in.

Aaron Dallas stood, holding his pencil as if it were a weapon. "Fear not, Juliet, I will rescue you from the dragon."

Mr. Bowman cleared his throat. "*Romeo and Juliet* isn't just about sword fighting. Who can tell the class what the play *is* about?"

"I know," Ken called out. "It's about two people mooning around in the olden days."

"No, that's not quite it, Ken," Mr. Bowman said firmly. "It's about love. And it's about family loyalty. It's also a story of betrayal. Shakespeare is also music, and we must learn to hear his melodies."

Jessica felt her heart flutter as she flipped through the pages, trying to find the musical numbers. She loved musicals and was really good at imitating singers. Maybe she should try to find the record to *Romeo and Juliet*. If she listened to it enough times, she could be ready to sing the part by Monday.

"What are you looking for, Jessica?" Mr. Bowman asked.

"I'm trying to find the lyrics to the opening number."

"The opening number?"

"I'm a great singer," she said proudly. "Unlike *some* people I know, who couldn't carry a tune in a bucket."

She turned and threw a significant look at Lila Fowler, who looked back at her scornfully. Lila was Jessica's best friend, but the two girls were fiercely competitive. Not long ago, when their school had made a video, Lila had insisted that *she* had to be the lead singer, even though she had a terrible voice.

Jessica wasn't going to let Lila beat her to the lead this time.

"That's very impressive, Jessica," Mr. Bowman said with a little smile. "But I'm afraid *Romeo and Juliet* isn't a musical. When I said Shakespeare was music, I was speaking metaphorically."

"Good one, Jessica," Dennis said sarcastically.

Jessica's face grew hot as the class began to laugh. She shot a desperate glance toward Elizabeth.

"Lots of Shakespeare's plays have been made into musicals," Elizabeth spoke up, cutting through the laughter. "Haven't you heard of *Kiss Me Kate*?"

"That's an old movie," Dennis argued, "not a Shakespeare play."

"Elizabeth is absolutely right," Mr. Bowman said. "The movie of *Kiss Me Kate* is a film version of a Broadway musical. And that Broadway musical is a modern-day tale based on Shakespeare's play *The Taming of the Shrew*."

Jessica tossed her head and smiled at Dennis.

"But there's never been a musical version of *Romeo and Juliet*," Lila said in a spiteful voice.

Jessica ground her teeth. Why did Lila have to make such a big deal out of this? Jessica had made a slight mistake. So what? It wasn't like Lila was any big intellectual, either.

"Oh, but there *is* a musical version of *Romeo and Juliet*," Mr. Bowman countered. "It's called *West Side Story*. And it's set in New York City in the 1950s."

He winked at Jessica. "I'm sure that's what Jessica had in mind. But the version we're going to do is the original, so there'll be no music or singing."

The bell rang and the class began gathering up their things.

"Take your scripts home," Mr. Bowman called out over the noise. "Read them and be prepared to audition next Monday, Tuesday, and Wednesday after school."

"I can't wait for next week," Lila said to Jessica as they walked out of the classroom. "I've always wanted to play a tragic romantic heroine."

"You mean *you're* trying out for Juliet?" Jessica asked.

"Of course I'm trying out for Juliet," Lila said,

flipping her hair. "Can you think of someone better for the part than me?"

Jessica glared at her. "Yeah, Lila, as a matter of fact I can."

"What do you mean, I'm not the Juliet type?" Lila demanded later at lunch. She and Jessica sat with the other members of the Unicorn Club at the Unicorner, their regular table in the lunchroom.

"Playing a romantic lead takes real talent," Jessica replied authoritatively.

"Are you saying Lila doesn't have *real talent*?" Janet Howell demanded.

Janet Howell was an eighth-grader and the president of the Unicorn Club. She was also Lila's first cousin, which meant she almost always took Lila's side against Jessica.

Jessica usually tried to avoid making Janet angry, but in this case she wasn't going to back down. "Not for something as important as Shakespeare," she replied.

"As if *you* know any more about Shakespeare than I do," Lila retorted. "At least I didn't think *Romeo and Juliet* was a musical."

Tamara Chase and Kimberly Haver started laughing.

Jessica pointed her banana at Lila. "Oh, come off it, Lila. You heard Mr. Bowman. He said . . ."

"So are you guys arguing over who's going to

play the lead?" Bruce Patman asked as he approached the table. "Why bother?"

Ellen Riteman smiled flirtatiously, and Tamara Chase ran her fingers through her hair. Bruce was one of the cutest boys in Sweet Valley Middle School. Jessica thought he was rude and conceited.

She squared her shoulders. "You're right, Bruce," she said, dropping her voice an octave. "There's no reason to argue. There is only one person who could truly bring Juliet to life and that's . . ."

"Maria Slater," Bruce Patman finished for her.

Jessica's face fell. She had forgotten all about Maria Slater.

Maria had been a professional child actress in Hollywood. Her family had moved to Sweet Valley this year, because her parents wanted her to have a normal childhood and a good education.

Just because Maria was a star doesn't mean she's a better actress than I am, Jessica reasoned.

"Maria's not trying out for any acting roles," Mandy Miller volunteered. "She wants to work crew this time, because she's never worked behind the scenes before."

"Then I guess the lead will go to you," Bruce said to Mandy. Jessica felt her chest tighten. Bruce had a point. Mandy was a really good actress, too. And she was so nice that Jessica hated to be competitive with her.

Mandy blushed. "Thanks, but I'm actually thinking of working on costumes."

Jessica felt a rush of relief. All her major competition was out of the way just like that.

She smiled graciously at Lila. "I'm sure there will be plenty of small roles for everyone," she said.

"Yeah, like maybe you could play the monkey," Bruce said, pointing at her banana.

Jessica put her banana down. "Very funny," she said. "I just hope you don't wind up playing Romeo."

"What do you care, Jessica?" Lila asked, tossing her head. "It won't affect *you* who's playing Romeo."

"Whoa, I don't want to be around for this one," Bruce said as he started to move off. "I'll let you girls fight it out."

"He'd make a pretty good Romeo, don't you think, Lila?" Janet asked.

Lila smiled. "Actually, I think I'd like Jake Hamilton for my Romeo."

Jessica rolled her eyes. "You don't know you'll be the lead. In fact, I'm sure you *won't*."

Lila's face darkened. "Wanna bet?"

All the Unicorns fell silent. Jessica cleared her throat. She hadn't exactly meant to sound so *certain* of Lila's failure, but sometimes Lila's bragging made her go a little overboard.

"Yeah, let's bet," Jessica said coolly. "Winner take all."

"All what?" Mary Wallace asked.

Jessica frowned. Hmmmm. Good question. Her parents wouldn't let her bet money. Besides, Lila was the wealthiest girl in Sweet Valley. Even if Jessica bet her whole allowance, it wouldn't impress Lila. "OK. How about *loser* take all," she amended.

"All what?" Mary asked again.

Jessica smiled wickedly. "All the face warts that Mr. Bowman has in the prop room. The loser has to wear a face full of warts for a week after the play."

"Good one, Jess," Mandy crowed as Tamara and Betsy high-fived each other across the table.

"Is it a bet?" Jessica asked, extending her hand toward Lila.

"It's a bet," Lila responded, giving Jessica's hand a firm shake.

Two

"*Go hence, to have more talk of these sad things,*" Amy read. "*Some shall be pardoned, and some punished; / For never was a story of more woe / Than this of Juliet and her Romeo.*"

She put down her script and gazed up at the ceiling in Elizabeth's bedroom. The girls had spent the past hour reading through the play out loud. "Wow! That's the saddest, most romantic story I've ever read in my whole life."

Elizabeth sighed. "I can't believe how beautiful the words are."

Amy nodded. "And the play's relevant to today, too."

"In what way?" Elizabeth asked. "How would the story be relevant to your life?"

Amy rested her chin on her hand. "Well, look at me and Ken Matthews."

"Hmm," Elizabeth said carefully. Ken Matthews was Amy's sort-of boyfriend, but Elizabeth had never thought to compare the two of them with Romeo and Juliet.

"Look at it this way," Amy continued, "Romeo Montague and Juliet Capulet were star-crossed lovers because their families had been feuding for years. The Suttons and the Matthewses have known each other for years and years. And you wouldn't believe how they argue."

Elizabeth laughed. "Your parents and the Matthewses argue when they play bridge. That doesn't mean they're having a feud."

"OK, OK. But yesterday, when Ken came over to borrow my math book, my mother wouldn't even let him in the house."

Elizabeth laughed again. "That's because your dad has the chicken pox and Ken's never had them."

Amy scowled in mock disappointment. "Gosh, Elizabeth. Do you have to be so . . . so . . . so . . ."

"So realistic?" Elizabeth finished for her with a laugh.

Amy grinned. "I guess so. Darn. I was really trying hard to make *Romeo and Juliet* relevant to my own life. I'm obviously not the romantic-heroine type." She threw Elizabeth a teasing smile. "But you are."

"*Not!*" Elizabeth retorted.

"You are too," Amy said.

"How am *I* a romantic heroine?"

"Well, for one thing, you have a boyfriend, Todd Wilkins. That takes care of the romantic side of the deal. And for another, you're always saving people from drowning and taking big risks to help others. I think that's pretty heroic. Put A and B together and what have you got? A genuine romantic heroine."

Elizabeth thought Amy was getting a little carried away, but she couldn't help blushing. "Todd is a *friend*. I mean, I like him and everything, but I definitely wouldn't want him hanging around outside my window at night like Romeo."

"Does this mean you're not going to try out for the play?"

"Are you kidding?" Elizabeth protested. "It's a beautiful play and everything, but I'm definitely not the type to take the spotlight."

"Then I guess you're not the romantic-heroine type," Amy conceded. "A true romantic heroine wouldn't let a little thing like the spotlight keep her from her Romeo. But I have to say, I can't think of any *real* romantics in the middle school."

Just then, the door to Elizabeth's bedroom swung open, and Jessica stood in the doorway. She opened her arms majestically and threw back her head. *"O Romeo. Romeo? Wherefore art thou Romeo?"*

Elizabeth gasped at the sight of her sister.

Jessica's blond hair rippled around her face and spilled dramatically over her shoulders. She wore a little crown made out of aluminum foil. One of her mother's chiffon scarves was attached to the back of the crown. And she wore an old black velvet pinafore that looked as though it was left over from several Christmases ago. She had pulled the hem out so that the garment hung practically to her ankles.

"Is that supposed to be a Shakespearean costume?" Elizabeth asked, trying not to laugh.

Jessica struck a dramatic pose and pressed her palm against her chest as she began to recite. "Romeo, Romeo, wherefore art thou Romeo?" Her eyes searched the room and then squinted at an imaginary horizon line. "One if by land and two if by sea and I shall stand at thy right hand and guard the bridge with thee. Give me liberty or give me death!" she cried, lifting a defiant fist. She lowered the fist and threw back her shoulders. "I regret that I have only one life to give to my country. But if I only have one life to live, let me live it as a blonde."

Jessica sank gracefully down into a deep curtsy. "Thank you, and make it a good day."

Elizabeth and Amy exchanged a glance and then burst out laughing. "What was that?" Elizabeth managed to ask through her giggles.

"It was Juliet's soliloquy, for your information," Jessica replied in a huffy tone. "Don't you think I'd make a great Juliet?"

"Um, well, that was a great delivery, Jess,"

Elizabeth said hesitantly as she controlled her laughter. "But it would probably be even *more* effective if you were actually delivering Juliet's lines."

"Yeah, it kind of sounded like you were making it up as you went along."

Jessica cleared her throat and grinned. "Well, as a matter of fact, I was. I haven't gotten around to reading the play yet. I'm just trying to get into character."

Elizabeth raised an eyebrow. "Listen, Jess, don't you think reading the play would help you get into character?"

"Yeah, whatever," Jessica said dismissively. "But I don't have time. Right now I have a *serious problem*. I just talked to Mandy, who talked to Mary, who talked to Janet. And Lila told her that she had already contacted a professional theatrical costumer in New York and asked them to send her a top-of-the-line Juliet costume. She'll have it on at the audition. Can you believe it? I'm a way better actress than Lila, but how am I supposed to compete with that costume?"

Elizabeth and Amy exchanged another look.

Jessica snapped her fingers. "I need velvet. Lots of velvet."

"Actually, Jessica," Amy said, "I think what you need is to read the play."

"Oh, come on," Jessica said. "This is the *theater*. It's all about *glamour*." She struck another dramatic pose.

Elizabeth laughed. "You might feel differently about that if you read the play. There's a little more to it than glamour. In fact, it's probably the saddest and most romantic story in the world. I bet you'll love it."

Jessica frowned. "But all those *thees* and *thous*."

"It starts to sound really natural once you get used to it," Amy assured her.

Jessica looked at the scripts on the floor with a wary eye. "It's pretty long," she said.

Elizabeth rolled her eyes. "It's really not so bad, Jess. Mr. Bowman marked the scenes we'll do in the play, so you can skim a lot of it. But you should definitely read the speeches for Romeo and Juliet."

Jessica sighed dreamily. "Oh, Romeo, Romeo, who would make a good Romeo? Rick Hunter? Or Aaron Dallas? Jake Hamilton? Or Tom McKay?" She smiled. "Yeah, I could definitely ride off into the sunset and live happily ever after with any of those guys."

Elizabeth and Amy started laughing again. "Jess, Juliet doesn't live happily ever after," Elizabeth explained. "She stabs herself and dies."

Jessica gasped. "*Stabs* herself! Why would she do that?"

"Because Romeo's dead."

Jessica widened her eyes. "*Dead!* What are you talking about? How did that happen?"

Elizabeth was laughing so hard she was practically choking. "Jessica! Don't you know anything about the story at all?"

Jessica shrugged. "Well, I know it's not a musical."

Elizabeth and Amy looked at each other, then at Jessica. "Read the play," they said in unison.

"Amy," Mrs. Wakefield said, sticking her head into the open doorway of Elizabeth's room at six thirty that evening. "Your mother just called. She wants you to come home for dinner. And Elizabeth, please wash your hands and come down for dinner and tell Jessica to do the same."

Elizabeth glanced at the clock. "Good grief. It's six thirty already."

Mrs. Wakefield disappeared, and Amy began collecting her books. "Thanks for going over that math with me."

"No problem," Elizabeth said with a smile. "It was fun."

They walked out into the hall, and Elizabeth knocked on Jessica's door. "Jess!"

"Come in," Jessica called in a strange, wobbly voice.

Elizabeth opened the door and gasped. "Jessica, what's wrong?"

Jessica's face was streaked with tears, and her eyes were red and swollen. "Oh, Elizabeth," she sniffled. "It's the most tragic thing I've ever heard of in my whole life. It's even better than *Days of Turmoil*."

Elizabeth and Amy looked at each other and grinned. "She read the play," they said in unison.

"So the story goes like this," Jessica said breathlessly that evening in the dining room. Elizabeth noticed that Jessica had hardly touched her chicken enchiladas, even though they were one of her favorites. She seemed too excited over the play to eat. "Romeo and Juliet fall in love at first sight," Jessica said. "But since her family and his family are bitter enemies, they have to sneak off and get married secretly. Then Juliet's father tries to make her marry this other guy, called Count Paris. Juliet knows she can't marry him because she's already married. But she can't tell anybody. Besides, she loves Romeo."

Elizabeth smiled. It was totally unlike Jessica to become so excited about something for school. And she could tell from her parents' smiles that they enjoyed hearing Jessica's version of the play, even though they already knew the story. Even the twins' fourteen-year-old brother, Steven, was listening so intently he'd stopped eating.

"So Juliet goes to this Friar Laurence guy and asks for help. A friar is like a priest, I think," Jessica continued. "Anyway, Friar Laurence knows all about medicines and herbs and stuff. So he gives Juliet this potion that will make her look dead for about forty-eight hours."

"OK, enough already," Steven broke in. "Quit making things up, Jessica. You're not fooling anyone. What kind of writer would come up with such a dumb plot?"

"Hmm, that's an interesting interpretation of Shakespeare's work," Mr. Wakefield said thoughtfully as he buttered a roll. "Not many people would call him *dumb*."

Steven shot his father a look and turned a little red. "You mean all this stuff about potions and secret marriages is really in the story?"

Jessica tossed her hair. "Of *course* it's all there. *I* know my Shakespeare. Unlike *some* people, who must have slept through the whole play when they did it at the high school."

Steven glared at her. "I didn't *sleep* through the play. I had a basketball game that night."

Mr. and Mrs. Wakefield looked at each other and began laughing.

Jessica cleared her throat. "What's so funny? Shakespeare's a really important writer, you know. I don't think you should be making jokes about him."

Mr. Wakefield smiled. "I agree, Jessica. Please excuse us and tell the rest of the story."

Jessica's eyes sparkled as she launched back in. "So Jessica . . . I mean . . . *Juliet* is supposed to drink this potion and look dead for a couple of days. That way, her parents have no choice but to call off her wedding and put her body in the family burial vault after her funeral."

"They bury her alive!" Steven exclaimed.

"Well, they don't actually *bury* her," Jessica corrected. "I mean, they don't put her in an underground grave. They put her in a vault. It's where they put the bodies of all the dead Capulets." She looked around the table. "*Vault*, as in a big marble building aboveground. Not a bank vault."

"Quit trying to score brownie points and get on with the story," Steven said impatiently.

Jessica scowled in Steven's direction.

"Don't pay any attention to him," Elizabeth advised.

Jessica's face relaxed back into a smile as she drew a deep breath to continue. "So anyway, Juliet's asleep in this vault with a bunch of dead people. And the friar tries to send a message to Romeo, who's been banished to Mantua for sword fighting, that Juliet's not really dead. The message tells him to plan on sneaking into the vault and waiting for her to wake up. Then they can run away and live happily ever after."

"Sounds like a plan to me," Steven said.

"Yeah. *Except that Romeo doesn't get the message!*"

Steven sat back in his chair and drew in his breath. "Oh, no . . ."

Jessica nodded. "That's right. When Romeo hears that Juliet is dead, he believes it. He hurries to the Capulets' family vault and goes inside so he can have one last glimpse of Juliet. After that, he drinks poison and dies so that his body can lie next to hers forever."

Steven dropped his fork. "But she's not really dead."

"That's the tragic irony of Shakespeare's tale," Mrs. Wakefield said in a serious voice.

"He killed himself for no reason at all," Steven protested.

"Wait until you hear the rest," Jessica said. "When Juliet wakes up . . ."

Steven gasped.

"She finds Romeo dead. She figures out what happened and stabs herself to death because she can't go on living without him."

"Then they both killed themselves for nothing!" Steven exclaimed in frustration.

"They didn't kill themselves for nothing, they killed themselves for love," Jessica corrected. She sighed dramatically. "It's so romantic. Which is just one reason why Juliet's the absolutely perfect role for me."

Elizabeth raised her eyebrows. "So it's not just about the glamour of the theater anymore?"

Jessica sighed deeply. "Lizzie, Lizzie, Lizzie. Of course I knew even before I read the play that I'm naturally suited to the spotlight. And now, after reading it, I realize I was born to play Juliet. She's just like me. She's young. She's passionate. She's committed. She's—"

"You're right," Steven interrupted. "Juliet *is* just like you. She's sickeningly romantic. She totally over-reacts. And she comes up with crazy, complicated schemes for getting what she wants. That phony poison bit is exactly the kind of hare-brained scheme you would come up with."

Elizabeth smothered her giggles behind her napkin. "You know, he has a point, Jess. You really are a modern-day Juliet!"

Three

Gargle, gargle, gargle.

Some romantic heroine! Elizabeth thought as she awoke in the middle of the night on Wednesday to the sound of Jessica's gargle. *Can't she at least close the bathroom door?* She turned over as she heard Jessica mumble something. Elizabeth couldn't help smiling a little. Jessica must be talking to herself. She made a mental note to tease her about it later.

As Elizabeth strained to listen, Jessica's words became clearer. She was reciting the balcony scene, where Juliet confirms her love for Romeo even though Romeo's family and hers are enemies.

O Romeo, Romeo! wherefore art thou Romeo?
Deny thy father and refuse thy name!
Or, if thou wilt not, be but sworn my love,

And I'll no longer be a Capulet.
'Tis but thy name that is my enemy.
Thou art thyself, though not a Montague.
What's Montague? It is nor hand, nor foot,
Nor arm, nor face, nor any other part
Belonging to a man. O, be some other name!
What's in a name? That which we call a rose
By any other name would smell as sweet. . . .

Elizabeth sat up in bed. She was so amazed at Jessica's performance, she forgot to be angry at her for reciting Shakespeare in the middle of the night. "Bravo!" she yelled. "Bravo!"

Jessica appeared in the open doorway of the bathroom that connected the bedrooms. "Does this mean you approve of my performance, fair Elizabeth?"

"Approve of it?" Elizabeth asked with a yawn. "Did you actually do that whole speech from memory?"

Jessica nodded. "I've been up memorizing all the major scenes from the first two acts."

Elizabeth gasped. "My sister actually stayed up late to do something for school? I'm shocked."

Jessica smiled. "Yeah, well, just because I'm beautiful and glamorous doesn't mean I can't be a hard worker when I want to be. I *can* work very hard when I really want something, you know."

"Believe me, I know," Elizabeth moaned. "And no matter what kind of crazy scheme you concoct to get what you want, I always wind up getting dragged into it."

"Not this time," Jessica promised. "There won't be any schemes. I know the lines. I'm a good actress. And I'm doing it all on my own with no help from anybody. What's to get dragged into?"

"Nothing," Elizabeth agreed with a smile. "You're right. For once, it looks like you're not going to need my help. You've already memorized a lot of the part. By audition time, I know you'll knock 'em dead."

"Thanks, Lizzie." Jessica walked over to the bathroom door, then paused and put the back of her hand to her forehead in a dramatic pose. *"Parting is such sweet sorrow. . . ."*

". . . refuse thy name! / Or, if thou wilt not, be but sworn my love, / And I'll no longer be a Capulet. / 'Tis but thy name that is my enemy. . . ."

"She's really coming along, don't you think?" Mrs. Wakefield asked Elizabeth. It was late Saturday morning, and Elizabeth and her mother were standing at the kitchen sink washing strawberries as Jessica practiced her lines in the living room.

"Yeah, she sounds really natural," Elizabeth agreed.

"What's natural?" Mr. Wakefield asked, bringing in the last two grocery bags from the car.

"We were talking about Jessica," Mrs. Wakefield

said. "Listen to her. She's really beginning to sound like a Shakespearean actress."

They all stood still as the words floated in from the living room.

> *What's in a name? That which we call a rose*
> *By any other name would smell as sweet.*
> *So Romeo would, were he not Romeo called,*
> *Retain that dear perfection which he owes . . .*

The glass doors banged shut as Steven came into the kitchen. He was dressed in basketball shorts and a T-shirt and he had a ball tucked under one arm. "We creamed 'em," he announced. "Too bad it was just a practice . . ."

"Shhhh!" Mr. and Mrs. Wakefield both said at the same time.

"What's wrong?" Steven asked.

"Nothing's wrong," Mrs. Wakefield answered. "We're listening to your sister."

Steven rolled his eyes but stood still to listen as Jessica's voice became even more intense.

> *. . . Without that title. Romeo, doff thy name;*
> *And for thy name, which is no part of thee,*
> *Take all myself.*

"Very nice," Mr. Wakefield said softly when the speech was over.

"Yeah, if you're into that sort of thing," Steven

commented. "I personally wish she'd act out a sword fight or something."

"You're such a romantic, Steven," Elizabeth teased. "Even you have to admit that Jessica sounds great."

"She's not bad, I guess," Steven said grudgingly.

"Well, *I* think she's fabulous," Mrs. Wakefield said proudly. "I can't think of one single thing that would prevent her from getting that part."

Concentrate, Elizabeth commanded herself as she stared at the page in her history book on Saturday afternoon. This was the fifth time she had read the same page from top to bottom, and she still wasn't absorbing anything. All the facts on the page kept getting scrambled in her head.

O Romeo, Romeo! wherefore art thou Romeo?
Deny thy father and refuse thy name;
Or, if thou wilt not, be but sworn my love . . .

Elizabeth jumped up from her desk and shut the door to the hall where Jessica was practicing. She had been hanging over the upstairs banister, pretending it was a balcony, and rehearsing her speech nonstop for the past hour.

Elizabeth returned to her desk and bent her head back over her book. But it was no use. Jessica's voice was softer, but the lines wouldn't stop drumming through her head.

It was like having some song stuck in her mind. No matter what she did, that song kept playing like a broken record.

Elizabeth went over to her bed and lay down. *Oh, well*, she thought. *There are worse things to have stuck in my head.*

"Where's Juliet?" Mr. Wakefield asked as he pulled out his chair and sat down at the dinner table.

"Last time I saw her, she was hanging over the banister and blowing kisses," Steven replied. "*O Romeo, Romeo! wherefore art thou Romeo?*" he imitated in a dramatic voice.

Elizabeth and her parents laughed and began applauding.

"That's great, Steven," Mr. Wakefield said. "If Jessica gets the part, maybe she'll let you be her understudy. You'd make a wonderful Juliet."

"Who would make a wonderful Juliet?" Jessica asked as she came floating into the dining room wearing her long velvet pinafore and her aluminum-foil crown.

She stopped quickly, as if she had just noticed that there were people at the table. She made a show of blushing confusion and then gave a low curtsy. "I bid you good evening."

Steven made a strangled noise in the back of his throat, and Elizabeth laughed into her napkin.

"Good evening, Juliet," Mrs. Wakefield said. "Won't you sit down?"

"With pleasure and I thank thee." Jessica pulled out her dining room chair and gracefully settled herself in.

Mr. Wakefield passed her the serving dish. "Won't you have some tuna casserole?"

Jessica frowned. Elizabeth bit her lip to keep from laughing. Jessica hated tuna casserole and always tried to get out of eating it.

"I thinketh nay," she said.

"I sayeth yea," Mr. Wakefield said.

Jessica's eyes cut left toward her mother, then right toward her father.

Suddenly she flung herself out of her chair and fell to the floor. *"Good father, I beseech you on my knees, hear me with patience but to speak a word."*

Mr. Wakefield gasped. Steven, Elizabeth, and Mrs. Wakefield all began to laugh.

Jessica threw herself in the other direction. *"Is there no pity sitting in the clouds, that sees to the bottom of my grief. O sweet my mother, cast me not away."*

"Sheesh," Steven complained. "All over a little tuna casserole."

Mrs. Wakefield was laughing so hard, she began to choke. "OK, OK, I give up," she said when she managed to get control of herself. "If you don't like the casserole, have two helpings of salad and go get some cheese out of the refrigerator to go with it."

Jessica gave her siblings a little satisfied smirk and hurried into the kitchen.

*　　　*　　　*

"O Romeo, Romeo! wherefore art thou Romeo?"
Jessica muttered quietly as she struggled to make
an aluminum-foil dagger.

She was sitting on the floor in front of the living
room television, and Steven lay sprawled on the
couch. They were watching *Teen Teams*, a game
show for teenagers.

"Deny thy father and refuse thy name," she murmured. As far as she was concerned, there was no
such thing as too much practicing. She planned to
be the perfect Juliet by Monday. And if she knew
Lila Fowler, Lila was probably spending all weekend parading around her house in her costume
from New York instead of actually memorizing and
practicing the lines.

Jessica twisted the point of her dagger to make it
more daggerlike. *There. This will probably go well
with my crown*, she thought. Juliet wasn't actually a
princess, but somehow a Shakespeare play seemed
to be just the right kind of show for a crown.
Besides, Lila would probably act even more like a
princess than she usually did, and Jessica didn't
want to risk being outprincessed at the audition.

Just then the doorbell rang.

"Are you expecting anybody?" Steven asked.

Jessica shook her head. "Not me."

"It's Amy," Elizabeth called out as she came
down the stairs. "She's going to spend the night."

Jessica went back to molding her dagger as
Elizabeth and Amy came into the room.

"Hi!" Amy said with a smile. "How's it going, Juliet?"

Jessica grinned. "Pretty good. Watch this. It's Juliet's death scene." She leaned over the business section of the paper that lay on the table and gazed into the face of the bald, eighty-year-old businessman whose picture took up half the page.

"What's here?" she began passionately, pretending the old man was her lifeless Romeo. *"A cup, clos'd in my true love's hand? / Poison, I see, hath been his timeless end."*

She lowered her eyelids. *"O churl! drunk all, and left no friendly drop / To help me after? I will kiss thy lips. / Haply some poison yet doth hang on them / To make me die with a restorative. / Thy lips are warm!"* Jessica lifted the newspaper and kissed it.

Steven began making a loud, smacking noise.

Amy and Elizabeth broke into laughter.

"I'll be brief," Jessica continued in a breathless voice.

"Ha!" Steven exclaimed sarcastically. "I wish!"

Elizabeth reached for the TV clicker and held it in the same way that Jessica was holding her aluminum-foil dagger.

Steven sat up quickly and grabbed a candlestick from the coffee table. He, too, brandished it like a dagger.

"O happy dagger!" Steven and Elizabeth exclaimed together.

Jessica frowned. "Cut it out, you guys. This is

the big moment. The most dramatic thing in the whole play."

"Then let her rip," Steven instructed.

Jessica cleared her throat as all three held up their daggers. *"O happy dagger!"* Steven and Elizabeth both recited along with Jessica in throbbing voices. *"This is thy sheath; there rest, and let me die,"* they all finished, with voices rising dramatically.

Steven stabbed himself and let out a long, yodeling scream as he tumbled onto the floor with a thump.

Elizabeth stabbed herself and then crossed her eyes, spun around, went rigid, and fell backward onto the sofa like a plank.

Jessica plunged her aluminum-foil dagger into her chest too hard and it crumpled.

Amy practically doubled over with laughter. "You guys are amazing," she choked. "How come everybody knows the part?"

"Are you kidding?" Steven said, sitting up. "If you'd been around here today, you'd know it, too. Jessica's been like a broken record. We've heard the play about fifty times."

"Well, it's really paid off, Jessica," Amy told her. "You sound amazing."

"Thanks, Amy," Jessica said, beaming. Normally, Jessica didn't place that much importance on Amy's opinion. Amy didn't know a thing about fashion or anything like that. But she was into writing and schoolwork like Elizabeth, and she probably knew a good Juliet when she saw one.

Amy dropped her overnight bag on the floor. "Speaking of the play, Maria and I were backstage to take a look at the sets and props. There are a few things we're going to have to replace—but face warts isn't one of them. I feel bad for whoever plays Juliet's nurse. Those warts are heinous."

Jessica couldn't help smiling. "I'll be sure and mention that to Lila on Monday."

Amy raised her eyebrows. "I thought she was trying out for Juliet, not the nurse."

"She is trying out for Juliet. But if . . . I mean . . . *when* she loses, she's going to be very interested in the face-wart inventory."

"Huh?" Elizabeth and Amy said together.

Jessica quickly filled them in on the terms of her bet with Lila.

"What an awful thing for friends to do to each other!" Amy exclaimed.

"In the theater, darling," Jessica drawled, "there's no such thing as friends."

"I don't know about the theater," Amy responded, "but it sounds to me like there's no such thing as friends in the Unicorn Club."

Four

Elizabeth gazed into Todd's eyes. He was wearing a pair of purple polka-dotted tights and a dinner napkin draped over his head.

Elizabeth was wearing Jessica's black velvet pinafore and a Los Angeles Dodgers cap. She and Todd were standing in the hallway of Sweet Valley Middle School, and all the students who milled around them had warts all over their faces.

This is pretty unromantic, Elizabeth thought. But it didn't matter. She had a message she was supposed to give Todd. A message from some teacher named Mr. Friar. It was a really important message. A really, really important message.

She opened her mouth to deliver it. "Romeo . . . I mean, Todd. Deny thy father and . . ." Elizabeth had to stop. Her voice was hoarse and it was breaking like a strange hiccup on every syllable.

She cleared her throat and tried again. "O Todd, Todd! wherefore art thou Todd?" Her voice was barely above a whisper.

"I'm right here in front of you," Todd answered in an irritable voice. "And what's with you, Juliet? Why are you whispering?"

Elizabeth's eyes flew open.

"Deny thy father and refuse thy name," came a croaking, creaking, wheezing voice from the bathroom.

Elizabeth sat up and looked at the clock. It was eight thirty. She had been dreaming. Dreaming that she was Juliet and Todd was Romeo and that the hoarse voice she had been hearing in the bathroom was her own. "Hey, what's going on in there?" she asked sleepily.

Amy let out a long, shuddering groan from the other bed. "She's been at it for the last half hour and her voice is almost gone. It sounds like she has laryngitis. I think you should tell her to cut it out."

Elizabeth pushed back the covers and padded across the floor toward the bathroom. She knocked softly. "Jess?"

There was a moment's pause before the door opened and Jessica's pale face peered out. "Yes?" she asked, her voice breaking.

"You sound awful."

"It's because I haven't been up very long."

"Amy says you've been up for half an hour."

"Half an hour's not very long."

"Jess, I think you're losing your voice."

Jessica shook her head. "This is nothing. All I need is to keep practicing," she said hoarsely. "The more I talk, the stronger my voice will be."

"I don't know, Jess," Elizabeth said skeptically. "I don't think it works that way."

"Well, I think you should save your advice for when you open your own acting school in Hollywood!" Jessica croaked before slamming the bathroom door shut.

Elizabeth frowned. Jessica could be moody, but it wasn't like her to be so snappish. And she was usually a zombie in the morning. *I'll bet Jessica's coming down with the Sweet Valley Middle School cold,* Elizabeth thought as she went over to her drawer and began searching for some jeans to wear. *And if she's smart, she'll give her voice a rest.*

Amy sat up in bed and yawned. "What's the plan for today?" she asked.

Elizabeth stepped into her favorite blue jeans. "Let's eat breakfast and then go to the bookstore and browse—unless you want to stay here and listen to Jessica recite Shakespeare in the bathroom."

"Not me," Amy said, reaching for her overnight bag. "I think I like my Juliet a little less froggy."

"What's in a name? That which we call a rose / By any other name would smell as sweet." Jessica croaked as Amy and Elizabeth hurried to finish dressing.

*   *   *

"Hello, Elizabeth. Hello, Amy."

Elizabeth immediately recognized Janet Howell's affected-sounding voice. She turned and saw Lila and Janet standing by the makeup counter in Kendall's department store.

"Hi, guys," Amy said cheerfully. "What's up?"

"We were just trying to make some decisions about Lila's stage makeup. Since Juliet is Italian, we thought Lila might wear some dark foundation and powder to make her look more the part."

Lila peered at herself in the large makeup mirror on the counter and studied her reflection. She sucked in her cheeks and stuck out her lips in a pout. "I'm definitely going to have to line my lips," she said decisively.

"Gee," Amy said with a smile. "I don't think Mr. Bowman really cares what kind of makeup you're wearing. I think he's more interested to see if you know the words and understand what they mean. That sort of thing."

Janet gave her a superior look. "Lila's not going to just walk onstage, throw out a few lines, and walk off, Amy. She is going to *become* the part."

"My costume arrived yesterday by special courier," Lila added smugly.

"That's great, Lila," Elizabeth said. "But don't you think it's a little premature to order a costume at this point?"

"I understand your loyalties to your sister, Elizabeth. But let's face it. I'm a better actress than

Jessica," Lila said, fluttering her eyelashes. "And I've been practicing with Tom McKay."

Elizabeth felt a little flicker of worry. Jessica had been practicing a lot. But she hadn't been practicing *with* anybody. That might make a big difference. "That's great, Lila," she repeated brightly. "I'd love to stay and talk, but we've got to get to the bookstore. Sale ends soon." She tugged at Amy's sleeve.

"Huh?" Amy grunted in surprise. "What . . . oh, *that* sale. We've got to buy some, ummm . . . uhhhh . . ."

"Bye," Elizabeth put in quickly, hustling Amy toward the door.

"Yeah, right. Bye," Amy called over her shoulder. "What's going on?" she sputtered as Elizabeth shoved open the front doors. "What are we doing?"

"I hate to admit it, but if Lila's practicing with Tom McKay, she might actually have a shot at getting the part. Jessica needs to practice with somebody. Somebody who can play Romeo."

"So we're somehow going to find him?" Amy asked.

Elizabeth let out a long sigh. "Her," she said, pointing at herself. She gave Amy a rueful glance. "I knew I was going to get mixed up in this somehow."

"Sheesh, Elizabeth, aren't you taking this audition a little too seriously?" Amy asked. "I mean, it would be a bummer if Jessica lost the part, but she'll deal."

Elizabeth sighed. "She'll deal by complaining about it for the next ten years. And she'd probably sooner die than wear the nurse's gross face warts for the week."

"They *are* pretty yucky," Amy said. "But Jessica got herself into this mess—why can't she get herself out of it?"

"Believe me, I'm not just trying to protect Jessica. I'm trying to protect *me*, too."

"Huh?"

Elizabeth gave Amy a sideways look. "If I know my sister, she'll somehow get me mixed up in her rotten luck. This might sound crazy, but I have a feeling I'll probably wind up wearing those face warts for her."

Five

◇

Jessica tossed and turned. She and Elizabeth had stayed up for hours practicing scenes, and now Romeo's *and* Juliet's lines were drumming through her head. She knew Romeo's part as well as her own.

Jessica wished that whoever was pounding on her head with a hammer would cut it out. She swallowed. *Ouch!* Her throat was so sore, it felt as if it were on fire. And when she tried to take a deep breath, she discovered that her nose was completely clogged up.

As horrible as it was to admit, there was no getting around it. She was sick.

Normally, she enjoyed being sick. It meant she could sleep late, stay home from school, and watch television all day.

But there was no way she was going to stay home and be sick today. There was way too much going on at school. She wanted to know who was going to sign up to audition for Romeo. And who was going to audition for the part of the nurse. And who else was going to audition for Juliet.

She lunged for the tissue box just as her head exploded in a huge, loud sneeze.

"Jessica!" her mother called from the hallway. "Did you sneeze?"

Uh-oh. "Do, Mob," she called. "Id wadn'd be." Oops. She cleared her throat. She tried again, forcing some air through her nose so she could pronounce her consonants correctly. "It wasn't me."

There, she thought. *I sound totally healthy.* Suddenly, the tip of her nose began twitching, and she felt her upper lip lifting. "Ahhhhhh-*choooo!*"

Mrs. Wakefield opened the door and walked to Jessica's bed. "Are you coming down with something, honey?"

"This is just allergies," Jessica answered promptly. She threw back the covers and swung her feet toward the floor, determined to be up and out of bed before her mother could ask too many questions.

Mrs. Wakefield put her hand on Jessica's shoulder and examined her face. "Allergies? To what?"

Hmmmmm. As far as Jessica knew, she wasn't allergic to anything. But lots of people were. What was it that guy in her math class was allergic to?

He was always talking about it. "Tomatoes," she answered.

Mrs. Wakefield lifted one eyebrow and put her hands on her hips. "Tomatoes have never given you any problems."

"Shellfish?" Jessica ventured.

"When was the last time you ate shellfish?"

"Strawberries?" Jessica tried lamely. "I had strawberries yesterday, remember?"

Mrs. Wakefield shook her head. "You might as well get back in that bed, young lady. Your eyes are red. Your face looks pale . . ."

Steven appeared in the doorway and stared at Jessica. "Juliet, Juliet," Steven said in a deep, Shakespearean voice. "Wherefore art thou's handkerchief?"

Mrs. Wakefield handed Jessica a tissue from the box beside the bed, and Jessica snatched it gratefully. "But I *can't* stay home," she protested.

"I wouldn't argue too much about it if I were you, Juliet," Steven said with a laugh. "If Romeo got a good look at you today, he'd hightail it back to Mantua."

Jessica grabbed a hand mirror off the bedside table. Yuck! Steven was right. She looked awful. This couldn't be good for her image as Juliet. She lowered the mirror and sank miserably back onto her pillows. "I'b sick," she admitted.

"And I suppose Jessica put you up to telling people that she's sick," Janet Howell said to

Elizabeth. It was a few minutes before third period, and Elizabeth was gathering some books from her locker in the hallway of Sweet Valley Middle School.

Elizabeth grabbed a couple of books and shut her locker with a bang. She whirled around to face Janet, Lila, and several other smirking Unicorns. "What do you mean *put me up*? Why would Jessica pretend to be sick?"

Janet sighed impatiently. "Please, Elizabeth, you're not dealing with amateurs here. We're all on to Jessica's plan. She's just faking being sick so she can stay out of school until Thursday and miss the auditions. That way, she can weasel out of the bet on a technicality—if she doesn't audition, then *technically* she doesn't lose. But you can tell her from me that Lila won't buy it and neither will I."

Elizabeth felt a flush of anger. "You don't know what you're talking about. The last thing Jessica's planning to do is miss the audition." She looked around at every face. "Jessica will be here tomorrow to audition. Don't you worry."

Jessica drank the last of her chicken soup with a loud slurp. She put the mug down on the coffee table, which was cluttered with a teapot, orange juice, aspirin, cold syrup, and tissues.

"Ugh," she grunted as she lay back down to watch today's episode of *Days of Turmoil*. She was so full of liquids, she could practically hear herself slosh with every move.

But she was determined to be well by tomorrow. And if that meant gallons of chicken soup, tea, and orange juice, then she would drink them.

She squinted at the TV screen. Flame Bennett, her favorite actress on *Days of Turmoil*, looked absolutely gorgeous. And Jessica had just read in *Soap* magazine that Flame had recently been sick with some mysterious flu. Jessica wondered if Flame Bennett had any beauty secrets she might be willing to share with her. Some makeup technique that could cover up dark under-eye circles and a red swollen nose, for example.

It was too bad she couldn't call Flame Bennett on the phone—actress to actress—and compare beauty tips.

"Flame?" she said into the elegant receiver of her French telephone. "It's Jessica Wakefield."

"Jessica, darling," Flame answered. "How's the most talented Shakespearean actress in Hollywood?"

"Stopped up," Jessica answered.

"Oh, no!" Flame breathed. "And the Academy Awards are tonight."

"I know," Jessica said. "That's why I called you. My nose is all red and my eyes have dark circles underneath them. Do you have any beauty tips for me so that I don't look like death when I accept my Oscar?"

"Don't you worry," Flame said in a reassuring voice.

"I'm going to send my personal makeup artist over to see you right now. She'll fix you up, and you'll look even more beautiful than I do."

Jessica smiled happily as she hung up the phone. Flame Bennett was her best friend, and she was much nicer to Jessica than Janet or Lila had ever been. She hoped Janet and Lila would be watching her tonight when she made her appearance at the Academy Awards.

Jessica squeezed her itching eyes shut and fast-forwarded a bit. Now it was nighttime. And she was sitting in the front row of the Hollywood auditorium at the Oscar ceremony.

Movie stars were sitting all around her, waving and blowing kisses in her direction.

Several TV cameras were positioned in the aisles and on the stage. All of them were turned toward Jessica, who looked absolutely stunning.

Suddenly, the audience fell silent. An elegant man on the stage opened an envelope and quickly scanned the contents. When he spoke, his voice rang out all through the Hollywood Auditorium. "The winner for best actress is Jessica Wakefield!"

The audience applauded wildly as Jessica moved slowly toward the stage in her elegant ball gown. She took the Oscar statue from the presenter, smiling at the audience with tears in her eyes.

The applause grew even louder.

Jessica shifted the Oscar so that it lay cradled in one

arm, then she lifted her free hand and waved at all her beloved fans. "Thank you," she mouthed. "Thank you all so much."

"What are you doing with my basketball trophy?"

Jessica blinked. "Huh?"

"What are you doing with my basketball trophy?" the voice repeated. "And why are you blowing me kisses?"

Jessica rubbed her blurry eyes. Steven was behind the couch, watching her. She was standing in front of the fireplace, having just received her Oscar.

Jessica folded her arms, trying to look as dignified as possible under the circumstances. "I'm practicing."

"Jessica!" Elizabeth called out from the front hall.

"Juliet's in here," Steven called.

Elizabeth came into the living room and frowned. "You should be lying down, Jess."

"She's *practicing*," Steven informed her.

Elizabeth grabbed Jessica's elbow and propelled her back to the couch. "You've practiced plenty. If you don't audition, Janet says you'll lose the bet. They won't call it off because you're sick."

Jessica groaned. Why did Elizabeth have to remind her of the bet when she was in the middle of receiving her Academy Award?

Jessica's image of herself in an elegant ball gown disappeared. A vision of her face covered with warts rose up in front of her watery eyes. "I have to audition tomorrow," she croaked, reaching for the cold medicine and the plastic cup that went with it. "I just have to."

"But I have to go to school tomorrow!" Jessica wailed. She was sitting up in bed at eight o'clock that evening, and Mrs. Wakefield had just finished taking her temperature. *"I can't stay home another day!"*

Mrs. Wakefield stroked Jessica's hair. "I'm sorry, honey, but you have a fever."

Jessica's tears clogged her already clogged sinus passages, and her hot forehead began to throb. She pressed a tissue to her face and let out a series of long, shuddering sobs.

"What's the matter, sweetie?" Mr. Wakefield asked, coming into the room. "Are you feeling worse?"

Jessica shook her head and sobbed even louder.

"She's upset about missing the audition tomorrow," Mrs. Wakefield whispered. "And because she's tired and . . ."

"I'm not tired!" Jessica shouted. "I slept all afternoon. That medicine makes me so sleepy I can't keep my eyes open." Jessica lifted her head and dabbed at her eyes. Both her parents were gazing at her with expressions of sympathy and concern.

Elizabeth and Steven appeared in the hall doorway and watched her with anxious expressions
while Mrs. Wakefield went into the bathroom. A
few moments later, she reappeared with a little
plastic cup full of cold medicine.

Usually, Jessica enjoyed being the center of attention. But for once she wanted everyone to stop
making such a big fuss over her. All she wanted
was to get to school tomorrow and knock Lila's
Juliet right off the balcony. "I have to go to school
tomorrow," she rasped. "Please. Please, let me go
to school tomorrow."

"Maybe you'll feel better in the morning,"
Elizabeth suggested.

Jessica turned her hopeful eyes toward her
mother. "Can I go if I feel better tomorrow?"

"Of course," Mrs. Wakefield replied. "But I
doubt that you're going to recover overnight."

"Maybe with a good night's sleep she will,"
Elizabeth said in a soothing voice.

"That's right," Jessica said with a nod. She
snatched the cup of cold medicine from Mrs.
Wakefield's hand, wrinkled her nose, and drank it
down in one big gulp.

"Yuck," she moaned, lying down and letting Mr.
and Mrs. Wakefield tuck her under the covers. She
was determined to have the most healthful sleep of
her life.

Six

Gross, Jessica thought as she stared at her face in the mirror on Tuesday morning. She was a mess. Her nose and eyes were red and swollen. Her body still ached all the way down to her toes. But there was no way she was going to let her parents know she was still sick. She'd set her alarm an hour early so that she could work on her face. If she couldn't actually *be* healthy, *looking* healthy was almost as good.

She quietly opened the drawer on her side of the tile bathroom counter and surveyed the litter of powders and pencils, lipsticks and concealers.

Hmmmm, she thought as she reached for a little vial of pale liquid base makeup. *OK, makeup, make me a star!*

*   *   *

"Did they use egg whites and library paste for makeup in the fifteen-hundreds?" Janet asked as she approached Jessica at her locker.

"Did they apply it with a shovel?" Lila added.

Jessica wanted to make a really nasty face at them, but she didn't want her makeup to crack so early in the day. Maybe she had gone a little overboard on the foundation and powder. But at least she wasn't blotchy.

"For your information, I've decided to go pale because love makes romantic heroines pale," Jessica said, tossing her hair and trying to ignore her throbbing head. "You see, I don't just *know* the part of Juliet. I *am* the part." She gave Lila a tight smile. "So you can laugh at my face today all you want. The whole school's going to be laughing at your face after I win the bet."

Lila's face darkened. "We'll see about that."

Lila and Janet turned and walked away, whispering together. Jessica had just turned to go to her first-period classroom when Elizabeth came hurrying around the corner.

"Jessica?" Elizabeth asked in an incredulous voice. "What's all that gunk on your face?"

"Don't you start in on me," Jessica ordered. "I looked so bad this morning, I had to do something. Otherwise, one of my teachers would probably take one look at me and call Mom."

"Speaking of Mom," Elizabeth said seriously, "she's about to blow a fuse."

"She found my note, right?" Jessica said. "I mean, I wrote that I was feeling tons better and came to school early so I could borrow somebody's notes from yesterday's history class."

"Yeah, she got the note," Elizabeth confirmed. "But she was still all set to march over here and drag you home."

"Home!" Jessica exclaimed hoarsely. "But I . . . ah . . . ah . . . ahhh-choooo!"

Elizabeth flinched. "I talked her out of it. I said if you were well enough to get out of bed early, you were well enough to go to school. But now I'm not sure I did the right thing."

"You did the right thing, Lizzie. I promise. I'm lots better. Lots, lots better. Ahhh-choooo!"

"Ahhh-choooo!"

Lila turned in her desk, gave Jessica a nasty smile, then faced forward and raised her hand.

"Yes, Lila?" Ms. Wyler said.

Lila stood. "Ms. Wyler, that's the fourth time Jessica has sneezed on me. I really don't think it's fair that I should have to be exposed to so many germs."

Ms. Wyler nodded. "I agree," she said. She smiled kindly at Jessica. "Don't think I'm unsympathetic, Jessica. I had the flu last week, and I felt awful."

"But I feel fine," Jessica insisted, throwing a dirty look at Lila.

"Nobody who feels fine sneezes four times," Lila snapped. "If you have the flu, you should go home before you give it to the rest of us."

"I'm not sick," Jessica argued. "I have allergies."

"How come I never heard you mention these 'allergies' before?" Lila asked sarcastically.

Ms. Wyler clapped her hands. "Girls. Girls. That's enough. Lila, you and I are not medical professionals. So I think it's pointless for the three of us to argue about this. Jessica, I'm going to write you a hall pass, and I want you to go to the school nurse."

"But . . ."

"No buts," Ms. Wyler said firmly.

"But . . ." Jessica began.

"No buts," the school nurse said briskly. "You're running a fever. The glands in your neck are swollen. And your tongue and throat are red and raw. You're going home."

She walked over to the desk, opened her student directory, and began dialing the Wakefields' house. "Mrs. Wakefield?" she said after a few moments. "This is the Sweet Valley Middle School nurse . . ."

Jessica felt a tear trickle down her cheek, cutting a track through the thick, pasty makeup. How could this be happening? How could she miss her chance to play the role that was *meant* to be hers? And if she couldn't audition, she would lose the bet by default. How could she spend a whole week walking around school looking even uglier than she looked today?

"But . . ."

"No buts," Mrs. Wakefield said. "You're going home, and you're going to stay home. If I weren't so worried about you, I would be very, very angry. That was a foolish thing you did today. There will be plenty of school plays in your future. It's not worth jeopardizing your health."

Jessica groaned and leaned her head back against the neck rest of the car. She felt just awful. But no matter how stuffy and feverish she was, she *had* to get to school before auditions ended.

"Can I go to school tomorrow?" she asked miserably.

"We'll see how you feel tonight," her mother answered. "If your fever goes away and stays away, you might be well enough to go back to school tomorrow. But I doubt it."

"Denny Jacobson, Todd Wilkins, and Jake Hamilton all tried out for Romeo this afternoon," Elizabeth said breathlessly. She had just gotten home from school and was sitting on the end of Jessica's bed, filling her in on what had happened at the auditions.

"I can't believe I missed it," Jessica muttered. "Were they good?"

"Denny was OK, and Jake was really good."

Elizabeth smiled. "And Todd was so good, Mr. Bowman asked him to read opposite all the auditioning Juliets tomorrow." She would never admit it, but seeing Todd in the role of Romeo had given Elizabeth a little fluttery feeling in her stomach. He had seemed so grown up and mature and . . . well . . . *romantic*. She had almost found herself wishing she could play Juliet opposite him.

"Never mind Romeo," Jessica said quickly. "Who auditioned for Juliet today?"

"Caroline Pearce and Ellen Riteman both auditioned, and they were both terrible. It was like they didn't have any idea what the words meant."

"What about Lila?" Jessica asked. "Did she audition?"

Elizabeth nodded and bit her lip.

"Well?"

"Well . . ." Elizabeth began uneasily. "She's not as good as you are. But she wasn't bad, and I have to say, her costume really added something. You're going to really have to pull out all the stops to beat her."

"How will I beat her if I can't get to school tomorrow?" Jessica moaned. "I'll lose by default. Ah . . . ah . . . ahhh-choooo!"

Elizabeth sighed sympathetically. She knew how much Jessica deserved the part. This case of the flu had come at the worst possible time. She wished there were something she could do.

Suddenly, Elizabeth hopped up and ran toward the bathroom.

"Where are you going?"

"To get aspirin, cold syrup, and the heating pad. You've got this afternoon and tonight to get well. Maybe if you devote the next twenty-four hours to your health, you can at least make it to the audition tomorrow, even if you don't go to school."

"Lizzie, you're brilliant," Jessica said, brightening. "You're wonderful. You're . . ."

"You're talking too much for a sick person. I command you to rest your voice," Elizabeth instructed.

Seven

"She's still got a fever," Mrs. Wakefield announced later that evening as she entered the kitchen, where Elizabeth and Mr. Wakefield were loading the dinner dishes into the dishwasher. Elizabeth felt her heart sink a little at her mother's news. "I'm calling the pediatrician's night nurse. I think I'll take Jessica to the doctor tomorrow."

She watched as her mother conversed with the night nurse. "Tomorrow at three thirty?" Mrs. Wakefield said. "Is that the earliest appointment we can get? . . . Oh, yes, I understand. I'm sure Dr. Grover is very busy. There really are a lot of colds and flu going around. We'll see you tomorrow at three thirty."

Elizabeth sighed as Mrs. Wakefield hung up the phone. Poor Jessica. There was no way she was going to make it to that audition.

Elizabeth loaded the last dish into the dishwasher. "Well, I think I'll go up and check on Jess."

"Good idea, honey," her mother said. "Could you tell her about her appointment tomorrow?"

"Sure, Mom," Elizabeth replied, tensing up. She wasn't looking forward to this.

As she climbed the stairs, Elizabeth heard a long sneeze that was followed by three short ones. *"Ah-choo! Ah-choo! Ah-choo!"*

She stuck her head through Jessica's open door. Jessica was sitting up, surrounded by pillows. Elizabeth had never seen such a pale and forlorn face in her whole life.

At the sight of Elizabeth's face, Jessica seemed to deflate. "Don't tell me. They're not going to let me audition tomorrow, are they?" she asked in a hoarse whisper.

Elizabeth shook her head as she entered Jessica's room. "You'll be at the doctor's office. Mom made an appointment for you at three thirty."

"It's not fair," Jessica croaked.

"I know," Elizabeth agreed. "It stinks. But Jess, even if Mom let you go tomorrow, you couldn't really audition. You don't have enough voice left."

Jessica's eyes began to brim with tears.

"If there were anything I could do to help you," Elizabeth said, "I would."

Jessica swallowed hard and her lips trembled as she began to cry. "I wouldn't mind losing so much if I didn't know, deep down, that I'm really, really good at the part."

Elizabeth nodded sympathetically. "You'd make an amazing Juliet. But look at it this way," she said, forcing a smile. "It's not a total loss. This family can now consider itself a lot more cultured. We all know the play by heart, too."

Jessica's head shot up, and her eyes snapped so brightly that Elizabeth practically saw sparks. Was this some kind of symptom of the flu that she didn't know about? But it really didn't look like the flu. In fact, there was something strangely familiar about the sparkle in Jessica's eyes. Something Elizabeth wasn't sure she liked.

Jessica gripped Elizabeth's arm. "Elizabeth, you're a genius."

Elizabeth was getting a little nervous. "Jessica," she began. "I don't know what you're . . ."

"*You* can audition," Jessica announced happily.

"Oh, no."

"You know the part as well as I do."

"Knowing the lines and being able to act aren't the same thing," Elizabeth said firmly.

Jessica looked at her pleadingly. "I know that you, my perfect, wonderful, talented sister, will be able to do this for me."

"No way, Jess. People would figure it out. Lila and Janet . . ."

Jessica flopped back on the pillow and moaned dramatically. "You might as well be on their side."

"Don't be ridiculous."

"You're all against me," she wailed. "Every-body's against me. Janet. Lila. You."

"I'm not *against* you," Elizabeth retorted. "Please be reasonable. *Please!*"

Jessica sat up abruptly and glared at Elizabeth. "Some sister!" she hissed sarcastically. "Two sec-onds ago you were promising to do anything you could to help me. And now, when I ask you to do this one, teeny-weeny, little . . ."

"*Teeny-weeny nothing!*" Elizabeth exclaimed. "You're crazy. I can't get up on a stage in front of half the school and pretend to be you pretending to be Juliet."

"Of course you can. It couldn't be simpler. Just wear your hair down like I do and wear one of my purple T-shirts."

Purple was the official color of the Unicorn Club, and Jessica tried to wear something purple every day.

Elizabeth glared at Jessica. She wasn't sure how, but Jessica was starting to make this crazy idea sound doable. She was going to have to be on her guard.

"You'd get to play Juliet opposite Todd," Jessica added in a wheedling tone.

Elizabeth felt a little flutter at the base of her spine, and her cheeks burned. *Keep a grip*, she or-dered herself.

Elizabeth shook her head defiantly. "Sorry, Jess,

but no way. Nohow. I refuse. I absolutely and positively refuse. N. O. No. *Non. Niet.* Negatory. Nay."

"Nay," Elizabeth said.

"Yea," Jessica corrected.

"Yea, noise?" Elizabeth amended. *"Then I'll be brief."* She brandished an imaginary dagger. *"O happy dagger! / This is thy shield."*

"Sheath," Jessica corrected.

Elizabeth slumped on the bed. "We've been at this for an hour," she complained, "and I'm just getting worse. And I'm tired of stabbing myself and falling on the floor. I'm getting a big bruise on my hip."

"We must suffer for our art," Jessica said wisely. "Now take it from *Yea, noise.*"

"OK, OK." Elizabeth sighed. She stood and held up her imaginary dagger. *"Yea, noise? Then I'll be brief."*

"No, *I'll* be brief," a voice said at the doorway.

Elizabeth and Jessica looked up and saw Mr. Wakefield smiling at them. He held up three fingers. "Three words—*go to bed.*"

"Dad!" Jessica complained. "I've been sleeping all day!"

"You need to sleep," Mr. Wakefield said kindly. "You too, Elizabeth. So I suggest you girls wind it up."

Mr. Wakefield stepped on down the hall toward the master bedroom, and Elizabeth fixed Jessica with a hard stare. "This is crazy, you know? The craziest thing you've ever made me do."

Jessica smiled. "But look what a great Juliet you're turning out to be. I knew you had it in you." She plumped her pillows and shook out her quilt. "Wake me up in the morning, and we'll consult on wardrobe when we know what the weather's like. If it's sunny, I think my purple gauze poet's shirt would be great. It's romantic and old-fashioned looking."

Elizabeth sighed exhaustedly. "Just out of curiosity, if I'm supposed to be you tomorrow, what happened to me?"

"Simple," Jessica said with a smile. "You came down with the flu."

Elizabeth tossed fitfully. She kicked the blanket off, sat up, and punched her pillow a few times. Then she lay down and put her pillow over her head.

It was no use. Those darned Shakespeare lines were going around and around in her head, and they were all a mishmash. A line from this scene. A line from that scene. A line from the Gettysburg Address.

Elizabeth sat up and punched her pillow again. *There's only one consolation*, she thought miserably. At least she wouldn't be making a fool out of herself at that audition tomorrow. She would be making a fool out of Jessica.

*   *   *

"Bye, Mom!"

Jessica awoke the next morning to the sound of Steven's voice.

"Bye, Mom!" she heard Elizabeth echo.

Elizabeth!

Jessica shot up out of bed. Elizabeth was supposed to have awakened her. They were going to talk about what Elizabeth should wear to impersonate Jessica at the audition. And now Elizabeth was sneaking out of the house.

She finked out, Jessica seethed. *I never should have let her go to sleep. She probably had too much time to think, and now she's having one of her play-it-safe, goody-goody, stick-in-the-mud, play-by-the-rules attacks.*

Jessica ran over to the window and looked down. Maybe she could call Elizabeth back. Give her a pep talk. Throw herself on her mercy.

The sky was gray and there was a light rain coming down. Jessica could see the top of Elizabeth's umbrella, but no Elizabeth. And she was moving too fast for Jessica to be able to call out to her from the window.

A sudden gust of wind snatched Elizabeth's umbrella from her hand and made her chase it down the sidewalk.

Jessica felt her heart leap.

Her sister was wearing a purple sweatshirt. And her long blond hair was blowing loosely around her shoulders. Furthermore, she had Jessica's purple backpack over her shoulder instead of her own blue one.

So Elizabeth had come through for her after all.

Way to go, Lizzie, she thought happily. *Just don't goof up and make me look bad.*

Eight

◇

I'm an idiot, Elizabeth thought as she hurried into the school building. *I'm a total and complete idiot. And a doormat, too. How did I ever let Jessica talk me into this half-baked plan?*

Amy came hurrying out the door of the girls' bathroom. "Hi, Amy," Elizabeth said. "I wanted to tell you—I'm running late on proofreading your story for the *Sixers* but . . ."

Amy frowned. "Elizabeth gave *you* my article to proof?"

Oops! Elizabeth fluffed her hair, trying to get into the role of Jessica. "I mean, *Elizabeth* asked me to tell you that she's late proofreading your *Sixers* story. She caught the flu, but she says not to worry. She'll have it proofread in time for publication."

Amy smiled happily. "Good. I know it's kind of

a sensitive subject. I just hope it's not too sensitive a subject to print."

"No way," Elizabeth protested. "Sure it's a sensitive subject with some people. But discovering you have a long-lost half-sister is a really compelling topic. I think lots of people will like hearing about how you and Ashley ended up forming a really close sisterly bond."

Amy frowned. "How come you know what I wrote?"

Elizabeth's mouth fell open. "Uhhh . . . mmmm . . . well . . ."

"Did you sneak a peek when she wasn't looking or something?"

Elizabeth's mouth opened and closed. "Uhhh . . . mmm . . . well . . ."

Amy smiled. "Don't worry. I'm just glad you were interested. I mean, I really wanted to write something other kids would want to read."

"Oh, I definitely think it's something other kids would want to read," Elizabeth insisted. Then she cleared her throat and flipped her hair off her shoulders in a sort of Jessica gesture. "Not that I'm any journalism expert," she said, imitating Jessica's clipped speech. "I'm more into the glamour professions—like acting."

Amy looked around. "Actually, Jessica, could I ask you a favor?"

"Sure," Elizabeth replied. "I guess," she added, remembering she was Jessica.

"Writing a story that personal makes me feel kind of vulnerable. And I know Elizabeth would never say anything that might hurt my feelings. So if you get a chance, could you see if you could get Elizabeth's honest opinion on my story?"

"I think I could probably find that out for you," Elizabeth said with a smile.

"Thanks. And by the way, I'm glad to see you're up and at 'em today. So far, Lila's way out front in the Juliet race. But she hasn't had any serious competition."

"She does now," Elizabeth said in a confident voice. But she felt an anxious flutter in her stomach as she waved and hurried toward the lockers. *The first bell hasn't even rung, and I'm already forgetting my role,* she thought nervously.

"Jessica!"

Elizabeth turned and saw Aaron Dallas hurrying down the hall in her direction. "Can I borrow your math book next period?" he asked as he fell into step beside her. "I left mine at home."

"Sure," Elizabeth replied. Jessica didn't have math until third period, so she wouldn't be needing the textbook herself. "I'll get it out of my locker."

With Aaron at her heels, Elizabeth hurried toward the lockers, where Lila, Janet, and Betsy Gordon were gathered.

"What are you doing here?" Lila demanded when she saw Elizabeth.

"I go to school here," Elizabeth quipped as she began twisting the combination lock.

"What are you doing?" Aaron asked.

"I'm getting my math book."

"But that's not your locker," he said.

Elizabeth felt a surge of panic. What was Jessica's locker number? What was her combination?

"Jessica," Aaron said, "are you all right?"

"No, she's not all right," Lila said triumphantly. "She's sick, and I think she ought to go home right now."

Elizabeth glared at Lila. "I feel just fine," she said, suddenly determined to regain her composure. She turned to Aaron. "I forgot some of my books. And since Elizabeth's out sick today, you might as well use her book."

She opened the locker, fished out the book, and handed it to Aaron.

"Thanks, Jessica," he said gratefully.

"You're welcome," Elizabeth said softly, throwing Lila a self-satisfied smile. *It's amazing how pretending to be Jessica has made* me *feel competitive with Lila, too*, she thought as she walked away toward her first-period class.

By lunchtime, Elizabeth was a mess. She had gotten Jessica's second and third periods mixed up, showing up for French when she was supposed to be in math class.

Even though she was starving, she knew she couldn't set foot in the lunchroom. She wouldn't last for two minutes in the Unicorner before Lila Fowler would sense she wasn't really Jessica.

Elizabeth shoved her books into her locker and tucked her script under her arm. Just to be on the safe side, she would spend her lunch hour in the library going over the play.

She sighed heavily as she walked to the library. This was shaping up to be the longest day of her whole life.

"Well, this is it," Maria Slater said to Elizabeth as they approached the stage door of the auditorium. The final bell had rung, and Elizabeth was so nervous about her audition that she was really grateful for Maria's company. "I checked the list. You're the last Juliet to audition. And you're up next."

Elizabeth's legs began to feel wobbly. "Will I be auditioning with somebody, or will I do it alone?"

"Todd Wilkins is going to read opposite you."

"Oh," she said, feeling her neck flush. She'd forgotten that Todd was reading opposite the Juliets. Todd was her sort-of boyfriend—which meant that gushing poetry at him was going to be embarrassing in a pretty major way.

"OK, Juliet, you're on!" Mr. Bowman shouted from the first row of the auditorium. "Act Two.

Scene Two. The Balcony. Take it from O *Romeo, Romeo! wherefore art thou Romeo?"*

Elizabeth leaned slightly forward, as if she were leaning over a balcony. She cleared her throat, cast her eyes over an invisible garden below and . . .

. . . nothing happened.

Elizabeth's mind was completely blank. She couldn't remember one word.

"Juliet?" Mr. Bowman prompted.

Elizabeth cleared her throat and tried again. *"O Romeo, Romeo?"* she began in a thin voice. She looked over at Todd and felt incredibly embarrassed. *"Wherefore art thou Romeo?"* Then, to her horror, she giggled.

Oh, please let me stop, she mentally pleaded. *Please don't let me get hysterical.*

But the harder she tried to stop, the more she laughed. Pretty soon she was guffawing. *This is horrible*, she thought, giggling furiously. *Absolutely horrible. I wish somebody would slap me.*

She saw Todd frown in confusion and Mr. Bowman stand up. "Jessica," he barked irritably, "if you haven't prepared properly and think this is all a big joke, then please leave the stage and let the rest of us get on with our work."

"S-s-sorry, Mr. Bowman," she choked, but her giggles were uncontrollable.

Then she heard a little buzzing whisper over the hyena sound she was making. She looked over and saw Janet and Lila smiling and elbowing each other. Lila gave Elizabeth a smirk.

Elizabeth stopped laughing instantly as she felt a wave of anger. *You think you rule the world, Lila Fowler. You're a rude, spoiled brat, and I'm about to put you in your place.*

Once more Elizabeth focused her eyes as if she were looking out into a starry garden. "*Deny thy father and refuse thy name! / Or, if thou wilt not, be but sworn my love, / And I'll no longer be a Capulet.*"

She heard several people around her gasp in surprise at the sudden transformation.

Elizabeth let her eyelashes flutter down, as if she were experiencing a deep and rapturous emotion. Then, she lifted her lids and cocked her head as if she were pondering a question. "*'Tis but thy name that is my enemy. / Thou art thyself, though not a Montague. What's Montague?*"

She stepped forward and opened her hands, as if she were experiencing a startling revelation. "*It is nor hand, nor foot, / Nor arm, nor face, nor any other part / belonging to a man.*"

Elizabeth laced her fingers together and lifted her clasped hands to her chest. "*O, be some other name!*" she begged. She held out one hand, as if in greeting. "*What's in a name? That which we call a rose / By any other name would smell as sweet.*"

Todd's eyes were riveted on her face, and they grew a little brighter as her voice and movements became more animated. "*So Romeo would, were he not Romeo called, / Retain that dear perfection which he owes . . .*"

Suddenly, Elizabeth understood why people loved to act. Something magic was happening to her. She didn't feel embarrassed to be auditioning opposite Todd now, because she wasn't Elizabeth anymore. She wasn't Jessica either. She was Juliet.

She took a step forward and held out both arms, as if to embrace the night. *"Without that title. Romeo, doff thy name; | And for that name, which is no part of thee, | Take all myself."*

"Bravo!" Mr. Bowman yelled. He shot out of his seat and began hurrying up the stage steps.

All around her, people were applauding and whistling.

"Look," she heard Todd say as he showed his arm to Denny Jacobson. "I've got goose bumps."

Elizabeth had never felt such a rush of joy and pride. Everywhere she looked, she saw faces beaming with admiration and enthusiasm.

She couldn't believe it. She had made the role her own. She had found a bit of Juliet in plain old Elizabeth Wakefield.

"Great job, Jessica," Mr. Bowman said warmly.

Jessica?

Elizabeth's heart began to sink slowly into her stomach.

Nine

"*All right!*" Jessica threw her arms around Elizabeth. "Lila Fowler is vanquished. Jessica Wakefield is the winner."

"Don't get too carried away," Elizabeth cautioned. "We don't know anything for sure yet. The cast list won't be posted until Friday afternoon."

"I'm not worried," Jessica said confidently. "Amy called here this afternoon looking for me . . . I mean *you*. She wanted to see how you were feeling and tell you she was sorry you were sick and missed *my* audition." Jessica grinned. "She said you mopped up the floor with the competition. Everybody around school is saying you're . . . I mean *I'm* sure to get the part."

Elizabeth felt a funny little flicker in her stomach.

It wasn't the flicker she felt sometimes when Todd smiled at her.

And it wasn't the flicker that she felt just before a math test or a dental exam.

No. This was a different flicker altogether. Kind of a stomach-achy-all-the-way-up-to-the-chest flicker.

Maybe it was something that she ate at lunch.

Come to think of it, she hadn't had any lunch.

Jessica went over to the mirror and sat down. "The doctor said my temperature is back to normal, and he gave me a shot and some more medicine that made me sleep all day. I feel lots better." She beamed at her reflection. "And it shows. Look at me. I'm almost as beautiful as I was before. I'll be a great Juliet." She whirled around to face Elizabeth. "The doctor said if my temperature stays the same, I'll be back in school by Friday. I can't wait to get there and have everybody gushing over me."

The funny flicker in Elizabeth's stomach and chest burned hotter. And suddenly Elizabeth realized that what she was feeling was envy. Deep, explosive, horrible envy.

Jessica turned to face her with moist eyes. "You're the best sister in the world, Lizzie. I'll never forget this. Never in a million years."

Elizabeth tossed and turned in her bed Thursday night. *I'm the worst sister in the world,* she thought unhappily.

She turned and stared out the window into the

night. A good sister would never feel the way she was feeling now—used, exploited, jealous, and angry.

A good sister would be thrilled that her twin was getting something she wanted so much.

On the other hand, Elizabeth *had* worked just as hard as Jessica had. She *had* been the one to go on stage today. She *had* been the one to have such an amazing audition.

But she knew she had no choice. She'd agreed to audition for Jessica. She'd have to hand the part over to her.

"Come on, come on," Jessica urged, pushing her way through the mob in the hallway.

It was Friday after lunch and the cast list was scheduled to be posted outside Mr. Clark's office.

Mobs of students seemed to be surging in that direction.

Two eighth-grade girls in front of Elizabeth began to debate. ". . . Lila was good, of course, but Jessica Wakefield was incredible. She made me believe in the character."

Jessica elbowed Elizabeth and winked. "Sounds like I've got a lot of fans."

Elizabeth smiled thinly. Her heart was pounding with nervous anticipation. She knew it would take all her courage to be supportive to Jessica no matter what the outcome of the audition.

"Excuse us . . . excuse us," Jessica grunted as she shoved her way up to the front of the crowd and dragged Elizabeth along with her.

As soon as they found themselves in front of the bulletin board, Jessica squealed. "I got it! I got the part!"

"Way to go, Jessica!" said Rick Hunter, a cute seventh-grade boy. "You totally deserve it. Your audition was awesome."

"Oh, it was nothing," Jessica said, coolly tossing her hair.

Nothing! Elizabeth felt her chest tighten.

Rick laughed. "Yeah, you're obviously a natural. I guess the audition was no big deal."

It sure wasn't, Elizabeth thought. *Not when I was the one who did the work.*

"Auditioning is the easy part," Jessica said in an affected, theatrical drawl. "Now the real work starts." She lowered her eyelids and brushed a strand of hair from her face.

Elizabeth bit her lip. *What gives Jessica the right to be so arrogant about* my *audition?* she thought resentfully.

"You've got some sister," Rick said to Elizabeth.

Elizabeth tried to smile. She tried really, really hard. *You agreed to audition for Jessica,* she reminded herself. *It's not fair to get mad at her now because she's getting all the credit. Get a grip,* she told herself as she scanned the rest of the list. When she saw who was cast as Romeo she caught her breath.

Jessica was going to play a star-crossed lover opposite Todd Wilkins.

Her Todd Wilkins.

*   *   *

Elizabeth sat in her room, staring glumly out the window.

All afternoon, she had had to watch Jessica preen, show off, and brag about playing Juliet. Jessica was on top of the world. To add to her excitement, Lila was cast as her understudy. Jessica obviously loved the idea that Lila was second-best.

Second-best, Elizabeth thought. *Just like me.* She was always putting Jessica's needs ahead of her own—even when there was something she really, really wanted.

Elizabeth took a deep breath and reached a decision. For once, she was going to put her own interests first. She wanted to play Juliet. She had won the role. And she had to tell Jessica that.

She knew it wouldn't be easy. Jessica would be upset when Elizabeth told her. But Jessica loved Elizabeth. And she had no idea that Elizabeth felt this way. *It's probably not fair of me to be angry at her when she doesn't even know how much I want to be Juliet,* Elizabeth thought. *I'll give her the weekend to really get her health back. Then I'll tell her Sunday night.*

Having reached a decision made Elizabeth feel better. Things were going to work out. She felt sure of it. After all, she and Jessica were sisters.

Twins.

Best friends.

Right?

Ten

"Best friends don't stab each other in the back!" Jessica bellowed at the top of her lungs on Sunday night.

"Best friends don't try to take credit for somebody else's work!" Elizabeth bellowed back.

Jessica's eyes narrowed and her face turned red. Elizabeth had never seen her so mad.

But Elizabeth was mad, too. *Jessica's counting on me to give up and let her have her way as usual,* she thought resentfully. *Well, I'm not going to do her any favors.*

"I worked just as hard on that part as you did, Elizabeth Wakefield," Jessica said. "Harder!"

"Yeah. But you didn't get up on that stage and take the risk like I did. You didn't risk making a complete fool out of yourself."

"If I hadn't gotten sick, we wouldn't even be having this conversation. You never had any interest in acting before. And you know why? Because you're too chicken to act, that's why. And you would never have had the guts to get up on the stage and audition for the part if you hadn't had me to hide behind."

"That's not true," Elizabeth retorted.

"It is too," Jessica countered. "If you blew it, who was going to look bad? You? Or me? I'm the one who did the work, *and* I'm the one who took the risk."

"Ohhhhh," Elizabeth groaned through gritted teeth. "You're impossible to reason with. You are so selfish it's unbelievable."

"Me? Selfish? *I'm* not the one who's trying to stab my sister in the back."

"Who's stabbing you in the back?" Elizabeth demanded. "I'm being totally straightforward."

"OK. Fine. You're stabbing me in the front, then. But stabbing is stabbing, and that's what you're doing. I'm not stepping aside, and that's all there is to it. Don't I have enough problems with Lila and Janet sniping at me?" Jessica drew herself up and jutted out her chin. "*Et tu*, Lizzie," she said in a tragic, disappointed voice.

"Wrong play," Elizabeth snapped. "That's from *Julius Caesar*. And the quote is *et tu, Brute*. It means *You, too, Brutus*? Caesar says it to his best friend after Brutus betrays him—not unlike a girl I know who happens to be a twin and who also happens to be named Jessica."

"So I don't know every line of every Shakespeare play," Jessica sneered. "Big deal. Neither do you."

"At least I didn't think *Romeo and Juliet* was a musical," Elizabeth said with a bitter laugh.

The door to Jessica's room swung open. "Girls! Girls!" Mrs. Wakefield said sharply. "What's all this yelling about? What's the matter?"

Elizabeth and Jessica both fell silent, and Elizabeth felt Jessica's hard gaze burning her face like a laser.

Elizabeth frowned. If she told their mother what the argument was about, Mrs. Wakefield would probably punish both of them. And Elizabeth had already had enough trouble because of Jessica. "Nothing's the matter," she muttered.

Mrs. Wakefield darted a look at Jessica. "Jessica, are you feeling all right?"

"I'm fine," Jessica answered irritably.

"Then why are you so snappish?" Mrs. Wakefield moved swiftly in her direction and put her hand on Jessica's forehead.

"Hmmm," she mused. "Your head feels cool. But I want you two to stop this shouting immediately. Jessica, you're still hoarse, and I suggest you go on and get to bed. And Elizabeth," she added sharply. "I'm surprised at you. You know how ill your sister has been. I think it's very foolish and inconsiderate of you to allow her to get into a shouting match."

As her mother turned her back, Jessica poked out her tongue at Elizabeth and made a nasty face.

Elizabeth turned and stalked out through the bathroom into her own room.

Juliet may have thought she had trouble, she thought as she flung herself on her bed in frustration, *but if she had had a twin named Jessica, she'd have known what real trouble was.*

"Ahhh-choooo! Excuse me," Jessica said the next day after second period. She was standing with a group of Unicorns, and she felt a little stuffy again.

It's all Elizabeth's fault, she decided. Thanks to Elizabeth she had cried for hours. Tears and lack of sleep seemed to have triggered a small relapse.

"If you've still got that cold, how did you manage to talk so clearly at the audition last Wednesday?" Lila asked her.

"For your information, Lila, I took a lot of decongestant before my audition," Jessica said.

Jessica turned her head in time to see Elizabeth coming toward the lockers. She looked exhausted, and her eyes were red and puffy. It was pretty obvious that Elizabeth had cried herself to sleep, too.

Jessica felt a small twinge of guilt. *Maybe I should have been a little more grateful. I mean, I did kind of stop thanking her once I knew I had gotten the part.*

Maybe she just wants me to tell her how great I think she is again.

"Hi, Elizabeth," she said softly as Elizabeth neared the group.

Elizabeth threw Jessica a smoldering and resentful look, then turned her head away.

Well, fine! Jessica thought angrily. *I wanted to make an effort, but obviously* she's *not going to even try.*

Just then Todd came around the corner, and Jessica reached out quickly and caught his sleeve. It was time to teach her back-stabbing sister a lesson. "I'm really looking forward to working with you," she told Todd in a sweet voice. "I've always thought you were a really good actor."

Todd looked surprised. "Really? How did you know? I've never done any acting before."

Jessica took a step closer and raised her voice to make sure Elizabeth could hear every word. "I just have an instinct for these things."

"Yeah, well, you definitely have great dramatic instincts," he said in a confiding voice. "That was an incredible audition."

Bang!

Elizabeth slammed her locker shut, and Jessica and Todd both jumped at the sound.

"Is something wrong, Elizabeth?" Jessica asked innocently.

Elizabeth glared at Jessica, then stormed down the hall.

"That's weird," Lila commented in a thoughtful voice. "Last week Elizabeth was really sticking up for you. Today it looks like she's not speaking to you. Are you guys having some kind of . . . *disagreement*?"

Jessica forced her eyes to meet Lila's suspicious gaze squarely. "Who, us?" She smiled. "No way. We're twins. Sisters. Best friends."

Lila's eyes narrowed again, as if she were thinking hard. "If you say so," she finally commented in a skeptical tone.

Eleven

Jessica hurried down the hall toward the girls' bathroom. She was already five minutes late for rehearsal, but she couldn't possibly be seen on a stage until she had freshened her makeup and combed her hair. She wanted her hair to have that tousled, romantic look and her skin to have a love-struck glow.

As Jessica artfully tended to her hair and face, she imagined the entire cast and crew breathlessly awaiting her arrival. After all, she was the leading lady, the star, and the show could not go on without her.

When she'd finished applying her lipstick and blush, Jessica affected an abstracted, dramatic expression and ran down the hall to the backstage entrance. She breezed through it, but then came to a skidding stop. Someone was reciting on the stage. Someone was reciting *her* lines.

> *O Romeo, Romeo! wherefore art thou Romeo?*
> *Deny thy father and refuse thy name;*
> *Or, if thou wilt not, be but sworn my love,*
> *And I'll no longer be a Capulet.*

"Very nice, Jessica." Mr. Bowman's voice came filtering toward her from the front row of the auditorium. "But slow down a little and be sure to enunciate clearly."

Jessica? This could only mean . . . Jessica felt her chest tighten as she tiptoed forward and peeked around the utility curtain.

Sure enough, standing onstage—*in her spot*—was Elizabeth. And she was wearing a purple shirt and her hair loose around her shoulders. Jessica watched with growing fury as Elizabeth finished the first portion of the speech.

"Nice," Mr. Bowman commented happily. "Now you exit."

Elizabeth turned dramatically and walked toward the curtain with her head held high. As she reached the area of the stage that was blocked off by the utility curtain, Jessica obligingly held the curtain back for her.

"Oh, thanks," Elizabeth said automatically.

"Thanks nothing," Jessica hissed, dropping the curtain and partitioning them from view.

Elizabeth's head snapped in Jessica's direction, and her eyes widened. "Well," she said. "I wondered when you would show up."

"I'm here now," Jessica said. "So you can beat it."

"No way," Elizabeth said stubbornly. "I'm here and I'm staying."

"Juliet!" Mr. Bowman's voice cried out. "You're back on. You missed your cue."

"Oh, sorry," Elizabeth and Jessica said at the same time.

They looked at each other. "Get lost," they said in unison.

"Juliet," Mr. Bowman called out impatiently, "where are you?"

Jessica threw her backpack toward Elizabeth. Catching it in her hands, Elizabeth fell backward from the momentum and landed on her seat with a thud.

Jessica fluttered her fingers at Elizabeth in farewell. Then she strode around the curtain toward center stage, where someone had done a chalk drawing of a balcony.

Jessica threw out her arms and planted her feet firmly on the stage. *And this is exactly where I'm going to stay,* she resolved. *There's no way I'm letting Elizabeth pull the same stunt twice. "Three words, dear Romeo, and good night indeed . . ."* she began.

"Why don't you take a break, Jess?" Mandy said. They were between scenes, and Jessica was sitting in the middle of the stage, silently going over her lines. "You look really beat."

Jessica had to admit that she felt pretty beat, too. She was dripping with sweat from sitting under the bright lights. But she wasn't going to take any chances. She was afraid Elizabeth was still lurking around somewhere—just waiting for Jessica to leave the stage so she could jump in and impersonate her again.

"I'm fine," she told Mandy lightly. "I just don't want to leave the stage and lose my grip on the character."

"Wouldn't you at least like to get some water?" Mandy asked.

Jessica squirmed. She *was* a little thirsty. But she was afraid to drink any water, because she really needed to go to the rest room already. And just the mention of water made her need to go even more.

She looked at her watch. One more hour of rehearsal. Could she last that long?

Mandy dug down into the pocket of her jeans and found some change. "I'm going to get a soda. Want one? I'll bring it to you."

Soda. Jessica groaned inwardly. Now there was no way around it. She was going to have to go. "No, thanks," she said.

"OK by me," Mandy chirped. "Be back in a minute." She hurried up the center aisle of the auditorium and exited through the doors in the back.

Jessica held her breath and listened carefully,

trying to detect any faint sound of footsteps or breathing. Nothing. There was no one around.

She stood up and tiptoed across the stage, careful not to let her footsteps echo on the floorboards. She slipped behind the utility curtain and followed the little hall that led to the dressing rooms. She entered the main girls' dressing room and looked around. It was full of boxes of wigs and costumes—but no people.

Jessica stepped into the small bathroom and . . .

Bang!

. . . the door swung shut behind her.

"Hey!" Jessica cried out. She whirled around and put her hand on the knob. But when she tried to turn it, it wouldn't move.

Oh, no! She was stuck. Somehow the door had gotten locked. Jessica pounded on the door. *"Help! Help! Can anybody hear me?"*

"I can hear you, all right," someone on the other side of the door replied.

Jessica's heart plummeted into her shoes. "Elizabeth?"

"Hi, Jess," Elizabeth said cheerfully through the door.

"Let me out of here!" Jessica demanded furiously. She grabbed the doorknob and rattled it with all her might.

"Don't worry," Elizabeth soothed. "I'll let you out—just as soon as rehearsal is over."

"You let me out right now or I'll scream."

"Scream all you want," Elizabeth said. "Nobody can hear you when the door to the hall is closed. Besides, you wouldn't want to give yourself laryngitis, would you?"

"*Elizabeth, you open this door right now or I'll kill you.*" Jessica banged on the door with her fists. "*Elizabeth!*" she screamed again.

But there was no answer this time. Elizabeth was gone.

Jessica's hot dry throat felt even hotter and dryer now. Elizabeth was right. If she kept screaming, she would just wind up too hoarse to speak.

She gave the door a last, angry kick. *Don't count on this happening again, Elizabeth*, Jessica thought darkly. The next rehearsal was on Wednesday, and Jessica vowed to be on time—even early. And she wouldn't have one single solitary thing to drink starting right after dinner on Tuesday night.

Twelve

"Jessica!" Mrs. Wakefield called out. "Dinner!"

It was Tuesday night, and Jessica lay across her bed staring angrily at the wall and thinking about every single rotten thing Elizabeth had done or said for the past ten years.

Why did everybody think Elizabeth was such a nice person? She wasn't a nice person at all. She was a terrible person. A back-stabbing, stage-stealing, kidnapping rat fink.

There was a brief knock, and Mrs. Wakefield stuck her head around the door. "Dinner, Jessica."

"I heard you," Jessica muttered grumpily.

"What did you say?" Mrs. Wakefield inquired sharply.

Jessica sat up and looked contrite. "I'm sorry," she said. "I didn't mean to sound so rude. I just . . .

just . . ." She wished she could tell her mother what Elizabeth had done to her. Maybe then her mother would see Elizabeth for what she was instead of thinking she was so perfect all the time.

"You were just what?" Mrs. Wakefield prompted as the frown on her face relaxed.

"I was just thinking about school and the play and stuff like that," she said. "I guess I'm a little nervous."

Mrs. Wakefield smiled. "Don't be nervous," she said. "I think being in a Shakespeare play will be a wonderful experience for you."

Yeah, it would *be a wonderful experience,* Jessica thought. *If only Elizabeth weren't around to interfere with everything.*

"Are you feeling all right, honey?" Mrs. Wakefield asked, putting her hand on Jessica's forehead. "You don't look like yourself."

"I feel fine," Jessica assured her. *If only I had never gotten sick in the first place. Then Elizabeth would never . . .* Suddenly, she had a brilliant idea. "But I think Elizabeth might not be feeling so great."

"Oh?" Mrs. Wakefield asked.

Jessica nodded. "She said she had a headache today—and that the glands underneath her ears felt a little swollen. But she didn't want to tell you, because she's got a big math test tomorrow and she's afraid you'll keep her home."

Mrs. Wakefield shook her head. "You girls have

got to learn that nothing is more important than your health."

She turned to leave the room, but Jessica snatched at her sleeve. "Please don't tell Elizabeth I told you," she begged. "She'll be so mad at me."

"I won't," Mrs. Wakefield promised. "But I'm going to keep my eye on her during dinner."

"So anyway," Steven said. "Joe sunk two baskets and Larry sunk three. We were up four points when . . ."

While Steven went on and on, telling some boring basketball story, Jessica sneaked the pepper shaker off the table and into her lap. *This will be just what Mom needs to see,* she thought. She poured some pepper into the little dent between the first and second knuckles on the top of her fist. When she was sure no one was looking, she quickly blew the pepper off her fist in Elizabeth's direction.

"Sheesh, Steven that sounds like ahhh . . . ahhhh . . . ahhhh . . ." Elizabeth fumbled wildly in her lap in search of her napkin and managed to get it to her nose just in time. *"Choooo!"* she finished explosively.

Mrs. Wakefield gave Elizabeth a long look. "Are you feeling all right, Elizabeth?"

While Elizabeth was busy wiping her nose and getting herself settled again, Jessica prepared for the next pepper attack.

"I'm fine," Elizabeth said, sniffling. "I just got

something in my nose and . . . ahhhh . . . ahhhhh . . . ahhhh . . . *choooo!"*

"Gee, Elizabeth," Steven said. "Maybe you caught Jessica's cold."

Elizabeth threw a suspicious look toward Jessica, then threw a resentful look toward Steven. "I did not catch Jessica's cold," she insisted.

"Hey," Steven protested. "Don't snap at me."

"Who's snapping?" Elizabeth snapped.

"Elizabeth," Mr. Wakefield soothed. "Your brother is just expressing his concern."

"Well, I'm fine," Elizabeth said, looking at her mother as Jessica sprinkled pepper over her sister's slice of roast.

Elizabeth turned her attention back to her plate and cut herself a mouthful of meat.

"Achhhhh! Hack! Hack! Hack!" Elizabeth clutched her throat as she coughed violently.

"That's it," Mrs. Wakefield said, laying her napkin down beside her plate. "Come on, Elizabeth. You're going up to bed."

"But I'm not sick," Elizabeth managed to choke.

"Sneezing. Coughing. Irritability. I'd say you've got Jessica's cold, and if you're not careful, it will turn into the flu. No more arguments and no school tomorrow. Now, let's go."

Elizabeth reluctantly put her own napkin down and stared daggers at Jessica. Jessica made her eyes look wide and sympathetic. "Gee. Tough break, Lizzie."

"Don't give me any of your . . ."

"No talking now," Mrs. Wakefield warned, putting her hand on Elizabeth's shoulder. "You don't want laryngitis, too."

As Mrs. Wakefield led Elizabeth away, Jessica hid her smile behind her napkin.

"OK, now Juliet exit," Mr. Bowman instructed.

Jessica pivoted and began wafting offstage with her eyes focused high over everyone's head. She stepped slowly, gracefully. Step. Step. Step. Step. "Oommph!" she grunted as she collided with someone offstage.

She dropped her eyes and gasped. "Elizabeth!" she exclaimed in amazement. "How did you get here?"

"Call it a miracle of modern medicine," Elizabeth snapped. "I took some aspirin, drank some juice, and convinced Mom that since I didn't have a fever and hadn't sneezed or coughed since dinner, she was overreacting. So now you can just step aside."

Jessica gave Elizabeth a smug smile. "I'm not stepping aside. But even if I did, you couldn't go on in my place. I'm wearing a different color sweatshirt. Mine's red and yours is blue."

"Guess again," Elizabeth said, giving Jessica back the same smug smile. She grabbed the hem of her blue sweatshirt and pulled it off over her head. Beneath it, she wore a red sweatshirt that looked exactly like Jessica's.

"Juliet!" Mr. Bowman called from the auditorium. "You missed your cue."

Elizabeth started forward, but Jessica took a step sideways and blocked her path. She'd had a feeling Elizabeth might try something like this, and she had taken precautions. "Not so fast," she warned. She grabbed the hem of her red sweatshirt and pulled it off over her head. She had on a purple T-shirt now. Jessica dropped her red sweatshirt on the ground next to Elizabeth's blue one. "I was wearing this when rehearsal started," Jessica said. "I didn't put the sweatshirt on until it got cold in here."

"Juliet!" Mr. Bowman called impatiently. "You're missing this cue too often. This is our last rehearsal for these scenes, and if you don't have it by the end of the afternoon, you're not going to have it on Friday night."

Jessica turned to hurry onstage but Elizabeth grabbed the back of her purple T-shirt and gave a tremendous yank. "Hey, let go!" Jessica ordered.

Just then Jessica felt the back of her T-shirt rip. "Oh no!" she cried.

"Oops!" Elizabeth giggled.

Jessica whirled toward Elizabeth in a fury. "I'll get you for this," she snarled, lunging for one of the sweatshirts that lay on the floor.

But Elizabeth grabbed the sweatshirts all at once and threw them upward and into the tangle of cords, wires, and pulleys that were suspended overhead. The bundle snagged in the web.

"If I were you, I'd run for the locker room," Elizabeth advised. "You can wear your gym shirt home." She fluttered her fingers at Jessica. "Ta-ta!"

Jessica could hardly speak, she was so enraged. Her whole body trembled with anger. Elizabeth was going to pay for this. She was going to pay big-time.

But first, Jessica had to go find some clothes.

Elizabeth is in big, big, big trouble, Jessica thought resentfully as she pulled everything out of her gym locker and started going through the pile of grubby shorts, shirts, and socks. *I can't believe I'm going to go out in public in this gross stuff. I'd like to rub her face in . . .*

"Hi."

Jessica spun around. Lila was standing in the doorway to the locker room.

"What are you doing here?" Jessica demanded.

Lila raised her eyebrows in surprise. "My shoes are giving me a blister, so I thought I'd come and change into my gym shoes while they practice the balcony scene."

Jessica glared at Lila. "You're supposed to be my understudy. And the understudies are supposed to stay and observe every rehearsal."

"*Your* understudy?" Lila looked confused. "What are you talking about?"

Jessica's stomach turned over. If Lila realized

that she was Jessica, then she would realize that it was Elizabeth who was on the stage.

"I meant you're supposed to be *Jessica's* understudy," Jessica said, affecting a polite, pleasant, Elizabeth-sounding voice.

Lila frowned. She took a step closer, studying Jessica's face. "Jessica?" she asked in a whisper.

Jessica took a step back. "You mean Elizabeth," she corrected.

"Do I?"

Jessica's face flushed.

Lila took a step even closer. "You know, I've had this feeling all along that there were certain . . . shall we say . . . *irregularities* in the audition process."

"Irregularities?" Jessica repeated. "I don't know what you're talking about."

"I'm talking about Elizabeth."

"What about her?"

Lila's eyes opened wide and she smiled. *"Her?"* she repeated.

Jessica cleared her throat. "I mean, what about *me?"*

Lila folded her arms. "I think that the wrong Juliet is onstage right now. And I think I could help put the right Juliet back in the part."

Jessica drew back. "You're just trying to get the part for yourself. And if you're so suspicious, why don't you go to Mr. Bowman and tell him all about it?"

Lila smiled slyly. "That would certainly create a lot of confusion and scandal, don't you think?"

Jessica did think. And if enough questions were asked—and if parents were called—things could get pretty sticky. "What do you want?" she asked grudgingly.

"To help you," Lila answered succinctly.

"Why would you want to help me?"

"I'll do anything not to have to spend a week wearing those gross face warts. If you'll agree to cancel the bet, I'll make sure that it's you who's up on that stage Friday night."

Jessica crossed her arms over her chest. "How?"

"OK, let's say for a minute that you *are* Jessica— and that Elizabeth is impersonating you. It's pretty easy to do during rehearsals. But what happens on the night of the show, when there's only one costume?"

Jessica felt her heart flutter uncomfortably. She had been planning to get to the dressing room first. But Elizabeth was turning out to be amazingly clever. She had probably already thought up some way to beat Jessica to the costume.

Lila smiled. "I ordered a costume for myself from New York," she reminded Jessica.

"So? What good would that do me? I mean *Jessica.*"

"Well," Lila said, dropping her voice to a conspiratorial whisper. "What I didn't tell anybody

was that the theatrical costumer in New York sent
two of everything."

"Two? How come?"

"Because professional costumers customarily
send two of everything—so the understudy can
have the same costume. That way, the understudy
can be waiting backstage and ready to go on at a
moment's notice."

"Where are the costumes now?" Jessica asked,
her heart beginning to pound.

"At my house," Lila said with a smile. "Where
nobody can get to them except me." She gave
Jessica a nudge and a broad wink.

Jessica's heart began to hammer with excitement. "That's it?" she asked. "All I have to do is
cancel the bet and you'll help me?"

"*Well*," Lila continued, "there is one other little
thing I want you to do." A sly smile creased her
face. "I think it would be nice if you had a tempo-
rary but very serious stomachache somewhere
around Act Two. That way, I'd get to go on for at
least a few minutes and have everyone see me in
my costume."

Jessica drew in a breath. Did she really want to
give a piece of the part to someone who'd been so
crummy to her?

On the other hand, Lila was offering her a
chance to sandbag Elizabeth once and for all. And
there was no way Jessica was going to turn it
down.

"So is it a deal?" Lila prompted.

"It's a deal," Jessica agreed with a grim nod of her head.

"Great job, Jessica and Todd," Mr. Bowman called after Elizabeth spoke Juliet's last few lines in the balcony scene. The cast and crew began to break up, but Elizabeth and Todd continued to gaze at each other. Elizabeth wasn't silly and boy-crazy like Jessica, but not even she could resist the warm and romantic bond the play seemed to have forged between her and her Romeo.

Slowly, Elizabeth and Todd began to walk toward each other as if they were the only ones in the auditorium.

"You did that scene beautifully, Todd," Elizabeth said quietly.

Todd reddened slightly. "You did a nice job, too." Then he frowned and shook his head, as if he were trying to clear it. "Let's not get carried away, though, Jessica."

Jessica!

Elizabeth was so surprised, she almost stumbled. She had forgotten that she was supposed to be Jessica.

"Todd!" Mandy called. "Could you come over here and try on this jacket?"

Todd walked away just as Amy came hurrying downstage with an armload of rubber swords.

"Hi! Any news on my *Sixers* article?" she asked, stopping next to Elizabeth.

Elizabeth shook her head a little as she tried to refocus her attention from Todd to Amy. "It's great," she said. "And I think it's really neat that you decided to share some of the things about your relationship that you told me in confidence."

Amy raised her eyebrows. "Told *you* in confidence? I didn't tell you anything in confidence."

"Oh! That is . . . I meant . . ."

Amy stepped forward and studied Elizabeth's face. Then she reared back and . . .

Clunk! . . . Bunk! . . . Clank!

. . . dropped the armload of swords.

"I don't believe it," she hissed. "It's you, isn't it? You're Elizabeth."

Elizabeth felt the color begin to drain out of her face. "Amy," she said quickly, "it's a long story, but I can explain."

Amy grabbed Elizabeth's arm and pulled her to the back of the auditorium. "Start talking," she ordered when they were out of earshot.

Thirteen

"Is the camcorder all set for tomorrow night?" Mrs. Wakefield asked on Thursday night at dinner.

"I got some new tape today," Mr. Wakefield answered. He smiled at Jessica. "We'll get the whole performance on tape."

Jessica grinned. "Videotaping the show is a great idea, Dad. That way I can watch myself over and over and over." She smiled brightly at Elizabeth.

Elizabeth smiled back.

Sheesh, she doesn't have to look so calm and satisfied, Jessica thought. *She's probably planning on beating me to the dressing room to get the costume on or something.*

Well, it was time to let her twin know that it took more than punctuality to make a star. "I had a very interesting conversation with Mr. Bowman today," Jessica said. "Instead of using the Juliet costume left over from the high school production, Lila Fowler is going to let me wear the costume she ordered from the professional costumer in New York."

Elizabeth dropped her forkful of chicken on her plate.

"Mr. Bowman was really excited about it," Jessica continued. "He said the costume would probably make the whole production."

"That's very nice of Lila," Mrs. Wakefield commented. "But what will she wear?"

Jessica smothered a laugh. "The costumer sent two of everything. One for the actress and one for the understudy."

"Oh, really," Elizabeth said thoughtfully. "Two of everything. That's interesting."

Jessica stared hard into Elizabeth's eyes and thought she detected a crafty glitter under the lowered lids.

"They'll stay at Lila's house until *just before the show*," Jessica said evenly. "The Fowlers' housekeeper is keeping them at Lila's so she can press them tomorrow. Then the chauffeur will bring her and the costumes to school just before it's time to go on. They won't be left alone for even *one minute*."

"What an odd remark," Mrs. Wakefield commented with a laugh. "What do you mean, *the costumes won't be left alone for even one minute*? You sound as if you're afraid someone might steal them."

"Ha ha ha ha!" Jessica laughed. "Isn't that funny, Elizabeth. The idea that someone might steal them."

"Ha ha ha ha," Elizabeth laughed.

"What about sneaking into Lila's house, finding the costumes, and hiding them until after the show?" Amy suggested after Elizabeth had filled her in on the costume situation.

Elizabeth shook her head and noticed that it had a strange, stuffed-with-cotton feeling. "No good," she whispered into the telephone. "The Fowlers have an alarm system and a couple of big dogs in the yard. Besides, neither one of us has any burgling experience."

At that moment Jessica passed through the living room on her way to the kitchen.

"Hold it," Elizabeth said quickly. She pointedly lowered the phone and covered the speaking end with her hand.

"Don't bother," Jessica said smugly. "I'm not interested in listening to you complain about me to *Amy*."

Elizabeth ground her teeth. Jessica thought she was so smart just because she had figured out who Elizabeth was talking to. For once, Jessica had been one step ahead of Elizabeth, and she was milking her little victory for all it was worth.

In the kitchen, Jessica began humming a romantic tune from Johnny Buck's latest album.

Elizabeth put the receiver back up to her ear. "Amy," she said in a low and urgent tone, "put on your thinking cap and think hard, because I've got to come up with some way to wipe that smug smile right off Jessica's ugly fa . . . fa . . . fa . . . *Ahhh-choooo!*" she finished with a great big sneeze.

"Elizabeth?" her mother called from the stairs. "I've heard a lot of those tonight."

"There's something in the air," Elizabeth called back to her mother. "I'm OK."

Mrs. Wakefield appeared in the doorway of the living room with a bottle and a large spoon. "I'm sure you are. But just to be on the safe side, I want you to take some medicine."

"But Mom, it'll put me to sleep."

"Sleep is exactly what you need if you're coming down with a cold."

Elizabeth sighed. "I'd guess I'd better go," she said into the phone.

"Go take your medicine and get a good night's sleep. I'll try to come up with some kind of plan. We may need Maria's help. Is it okay to fill her in?"

"Sure," Elizabeth answered. "Two heads are better than one."

"Yeah," Amy said. "But two Juliets is one too many."

"Ahhhh-choooo!" Elizabeth sneezed so hard during breakfast that Steven ducked his head on his side of table.

"Watch where you aim that thing," he said grumpily.

"Sorry," Elizabeth muttered, pulling a tissue from her pocket.

Mrs. Wakefield reached came over and felt Elizabeth's forehead. "You don't have any fever. But I wonder if you should stay home today."

"I feel fine," Elizabeth insisted. "I can go to school, no problem." It wasn't a complete lie. She did feel better than she had felt last night. Maybe it was because the cold medicine had made her sleep so soundly.

Mrs. Wakefield reached for the medicine bottle. "OK, but why don't you take a spoonful of this before you go? It will keep you from stuffing up."

Elizabeth shook her head. "It'll make me too sleepy. And I need to be on my toes today." She shot a look at Jessica and felt a little flicker of triumph. Jessica didn't look so smug now. She actually looked a little worried.

Good, Elizabeth thought. *She should be worried. Because this is war.*

Fourteen

"En garde!" Alex Betner shouted as Jessica and Mandy made their way down the hall before fifth period. He lifted his ruler and flourished it like a sword.

Mandy and Jessica began to giggle as several of the boys and some of the girls pulled their own rulers from their backpacks. Soon, it seemed as if everyone in the hallway was involved in a sword fight.

"Everyone's really psyched up for tonight," Mandy said. "It's like our mini-production is a bigger deal than the drama department's full-scale production of *My Fair Lady*."

"Well, they should be excited," Jessica said happily. "I have a feeling that tonight's going to be the biggest event of the year."

Just then she caught sight of Elizabeth, Amy, and Maria standing at the opposite end of the hall. And that sight made the weird feeling she'd had in her stomach that morning at breakfast come back.

She tossed her hair, trying to brush the feeling away. After all, there was no reason for her to be worried. She had covered every base. She was going to stop by home after school and then go straight to Lila's house at four thirty. At five thirty, the chauffeur would drive Lila, Jessica, and the costumes to school. Elizabeth was finished. Washed up. Out of the picture. Finito.

And Elizabeth knew it, too.

So what is she whispering about with Amy and Maria?

"Mom," Jessica said, hovering in the doorway of the kitchen after school, "where's Elizabeth?"

Mrs. Wakefield looked up from the sink where she was repotting some pansies. "She left a little while ago for Amy's. She said the two of them were going to go over to the school auditorium early to help out with the scenery."

Jessica felt her stomach give an uneasy lurch. She had hoped that Elizabeth would be at home up until the time she had to leave for Lila's. Jessica wanted to keep tabs on her.

She took a deep breath. *Relax,* she commanded herself. There was no way Elizabeth could get her hands on the costumes. No way in the world. So what was she worrying about?

"Look at this," Mrs. Wakefield said, reaching for a bottle of cold medicine. "Elizabeth forgot to take this with her. She said she was feeling a lot better, but I wanted her to have this on hand in case she got stuffy." She looked at Jessica. "Will you take this with you and give it to her? I'm sure you'll see Elizabeth at school before we will."

Jessica nodded. "Sure." *Although Elizabeth isn't going to take this stuff. She'll say it'll just make her . . .*

. . . fall asleep.

Jessica looked at the bottle of cold medicine her mother had handed her. Cold medicine would make Elizabeth fall asleep. An intriguing idea.

"But soft! what light through yonder window breaks? / It is the East, and Juliet is the sun! / Arise, fair sun, and kill the envious moon . . ."

Elizabeth was standing backstage and watching Todd as he nervously paced back and forth, practicing his lines. His face looked pale, and Elizabeth hoped he wasn't feeling sick. His understudy, Tom McKay, was at home with the flu that had been going around, so if Todd got too sick to go on, the play would be canceled. Without him, there wouldn't be a Romeo.

Elizabeth scribbled a few notes on the little pad she held in her hand so that Amy and Maria would know she was Elizabeth and not Jessica. She had made sure that she was dressed almost identically to Jessica, in a green T-shirt and jeans.

She cast a nervous look around for Amy and Maria. It was pandemonium backstage, but she spotted Amy on the other side of the stage and signaled her with a wave. Amy waved back, letting her know that she and Maria were ready.

"Hey, which is the rope that operates the main curtain again?" Brooke Dennis asked.

"That one," Randy Mason said, pointing.

"No, not *that* one," Lloyd Benson argued. "It's *that* one."

"Are you kidding? Where've you been? We've gone over this a million times. It's—"

"Watch out," Sarah Thomas squeaked as her stepsister, Sophia Rizzo, brushed past her pushing a large burial vault made of cardboard.

"Help, somebody!" yelled Dennis Cookman, who had agreed to play the nurse for extra credit when all the girls refused. "These warts keep falling off my face."

He really does look like an old, fat governess, Elizabeth thought as she examined the nurse's wig and billowing dress.

"Todd," Mandy called out from the other side of the stage. "You'd better get into your costume and let me make sure the Velcro fasteners will hold."

Looking fear-stricken, Todd gulped and lurched past Elizabeth in Mandy's direction.

Elizabeth looked anxiously at her watch. The

curtain was due to go up in ten minutes. Jessica was really cutting it down to the wire.

Elizabeth left the stage and walked out to the hallway. There was a sudden commotion at the end of that hall, and suddenly the double doors on the far side that opened onto the parking lot burst open.

Elizabeth ran back to the backstage door. "Here they come," she hissed at Amy. "Find Maria."

Amy disappeared into one of the many layers partitioned off by the curtains. When she emerged, she and Maria were pushing a large piece of scenery covered with a big canvas drop cloth.

The three girls raced toward the door and hovered outside the hall that led to the "star" dressing room.

Jessica and Lila were marching toward the dressing room door, rolling a rack on which two brightly colored velvet dresses billowed out.

For a moment Elizabeth stared, mesmerized. The dresses were absolutely beautiful, full of intricate embroidery. And she'd never seen so much material on a single piece of clothing in her life.

"Get down," Amy warned Elizabeth, removing the canvas drop cloth from the balcony set, which she and Maria were holding. "Here they come."

Lila and Jessica came speeding down the hall, making a beeline for the dressing room.

"Countdown to zero hour," Amy murmured, tightening her grip on the balcony set.

"Ten . . ." Maria began. "Nine . . . eight . . ."

There was the scuffling of footsteps as Elizabeth positioned herself.

Whirrrr! The rolling rack was closer now.

"Three . . ." Maria continued. "Two . . . one . . ."

"Let's do it," Amy commanded.

Maria gave a tremendous shove from her end, and Amy gave her side of the set a pull.

"Look out!" Amy cried as the rolling rack and the scenery collided.

"Hey!" Lila cried as she fell to the floor. The two billowing dresses fell off the rack and plopped down over her head like the silk of a parachute.

"Yikes!" Jessica yelled as Maria yanked her arm, shoving her headfirst into the deep bucket attached to the balcony set.

Phoomp! went the canvas drop cloth as Amy threw it over the balcony to hide Jessica's kicking feet.

"What's going on?" she demanded in a muffled voice from inside the bucket. "Get me up. Help me!"

Give it up, Jess, Elizabeth thought. *Everyone's too excited about the play to pay any attention to you.*

Elizabeth pitched her pad and pencil as Amy and Maria whisked the balcony to the other side of the stage.

"Hey!" Lila cried as she struggled beneath the velvet skirts of the dresses. "What's going on out there?"

Elizabeth held out her hand to hoist Lila to her feet. "That Amy Sutton is so clumsy," Elizabeth said in her best Jessica voice. "I don't know why it's so hard for her to watch where she's going. Here, Lila. Let me hang up the dresses. There. Now, let's hurry. We're already late."

Elizabeth's hands were shaking as she buttoned up the tiny pearl buttons that closed the fitted bodice of her Juliet costume. *Her* Juliet costume. She could hardly believe she was wearing something so beautiful. And she could hardly believe she was about to get onstage and play the part she had longed to play.

"Well, we did it," Lila said, buttoning her own dress and tying the little jeweled cap on her head. "We actually outsmarted Elizabeth."

Elizabeth felt the corner of her mouth twitch.

There was a knock on the door.

"Come in," she cried.

The door opened, and Todd stood there wearing a peplum jacket and pantaloons. Elizabeth couldn't help letting out a sigh. He looked very handsome. "Hi, Todd," she said shyly.

Todd blushed. "Ummm, Jessica," he stuttered, "could I talk to you for a moment?" He shot a look at Lila. "Privately?"

Elizabeth furrowed her brow. "Sure, Todd." She took his arm and the two of them retreated a few steps into the hallway.

"Uhhh, Jessica," he began, "this is kind of embarrassing to talk about. But I've got a cold coming
on. My throat's real sore and my ears are popping."

"Oh, no!" Elizabeth cried.

"Don't worry. I'll get through the show. But I
just thought that maybe when we . . . when we . . .
when we . . ."

"When we . . . what?"

"When we . . ." Todd lowered his voice. ". . .
kiss . . . um, that is, I think it might be better if
you kiss me on the cheek instead of . . . instead of
on the lips. That way you won't catch my cold."

Elizabeth felt her cheeks flushing beet red.
What am I supposed to say? she wondered, feeling
incredibly embarrassed. Then she remembered
that she wasn't Elizabeth. She was Jessica. And
Jessica wasn't embarrassed to talk about things
like kissing.

She forced herself to smile. "Sure, Todd. I'll kiss
you just like this." Elizabeth leaned forward and
kissed him softly on the cheek.

Todd looked startled.

Elizabeth laughed flirtatiously. "Is that the kind
of kiss you meant?"

He stepped back and swallowed hard. "Yeah.
Right. I mean, sure. That was fine. Not fine, I mean,
it was nice—not that I liked it—I mean, it's not that
I didn't like it . . . I just . . ."

"Hey, you guys, are you all set?" Mandy asked,
appearing at the dressing room door.

"We're ready," Elizabeth replied, turning gratefully away from the stammering Todd.

Mandy gazed at the Juliet costume. "Beautiful," she said breathlessly. "You're a gorgeous Juliet."

"Thanks," Elizabeth whispered, her heart thumping with anticipation.

Mandy smiled. "Five minutes to show time. And good luck."

"We'd better get over to the other side of the stage," Todd said. Elizabeth nodded and hurried away behind him.

"Where is it?" Jessica demanded, racing into the dressing room just as Lila was straightening her little jeweled cap on her head. "Where's my costume?"

Lila whirled around and her eyes grew large.

"Lila!" Jessica cried. "Don't just stand there staring at me. Where's my costume?"

Lila's lips opened and closed a few times.

"Lila! Answer me. What's the matter with you?"

"I thought you were wearing your costume," Lila croaked.

"Why would you think I was . . ." Jessica broke off as a horrible, sickening feeling hit her right in the ribs. Her own eyes grew wide with horror. "*Oh, nooo!*" she wailed. "You didn't. You didn't. Please tell me that you didn't give Elizabeth my costume."

Lila pulled a handful of her hair with frustration. "I didn't know it was her. I thought it was you. What happened?"

"What happened is my back-stabbing sister and her dirty, double-crossing friends tricked us, that's what," Jessica said angrily.

Lila groaned and buried her face in her hands. "This is horrible. Just—"

"Give me your costume," Jessica said suddenly, snatching Lila's sleeve.

"What?" Lila lifted her face.

"Quick. The curtain goes up in two minutes."

Lila snatched her sleeve away. "Forget it. It's my costume, and I want to wear it."

"Face warts, Lila," Jessica said in an ominous tone. "Face warts."

Lila stamped her foot and stubbornly set her jaw in defiance.

Jessica pointed to Lila's cheek. "I think a big one riiiight *there*."

Lila groaned again. "OK. Fine. You win."

Lila's fingers flew down the front of the dress, and within moments Lila was back in her jeans and T-shirt and Jessica was sumptuously arrayed in velvet and brocade.

"I still don't see how you're going to beat her onstage," Lila said sullenly.

"Are you kidding? Juliet's got a million exits and entrances. I'll get my chance. But you can help."

"Why should I help you any more than I already have?" Lila grumbled.

"Do I really need to remind you?" Jessica asked.

"What do you want me to do?" Lila asked grudgingly.

Jessica reached into her backpack and pulled out the bottle of cold medicine. She filled the plastic cup that came with it.

"What's that?" Lila asked.

"It's Elizabeth's cold medicine," Jessica answered. "Get a soda from the machine in the hall. Pour a little of the soda out, and then pour this medicine in. Shake it so that it mixes in with the soda. Then give it to Mandy and tell her it's for the tickle in *Jessica's* throat. We're going to turn Juliet into Sleeping Beauty. Now, go!"

Fifteen

◇

"Vial of poison. Check! Knife, swords, goblets, and masks. Check!" Amy muttered as she took inventory of the props, trying to calm her nerves.

"Hey, Amy," Mandy said, appearing at her elbow. "Lila says this is for Jessica." She handed Amy a cold can of soda. "It's to help the tickle in her throat. She'll have to gulp it down fast, though. Curtain goes up in twenty seconds."

Amy nodded distractedly as Mandy ran out. She rearranged the vial of poison on the table and took the soda can to give it to . . .

Wait a minute. Amy frowned. Who had the tickle in their throat? Jessica or Elizabeth?

Jessica was over her cold, wasn't she? And Elizabeth hadn't said anything to Amy about having a problem with her throat.

Amy heard a rasping, coughing sound behind her. She turned and saw Todd nervously massaging his throat. "Uh-oh," she said. "Have you got a cough?"

Todd nodded unhappily. "I'm really not feeling well." He forced a smile. "But the show must go on, right?" He coughed again.

"Here," Amy said, making a quick decision. "Drink this. It'll take the tickle out of your throat."

Todd gratefully grasped the soda and raised it to his mouth. "Ahhhh," he said, lowering the empty can and smacking his lips. "That felt really good."

"Places," a voice cried out. "Places, everybody. The house lights are going down right now." There was a rustle and stir backstage as Mr. Bowman herded the cast and crew toward the front of the stage.

Amy peeked around the corner of the main curtain and saw that the house was full. Mr. and Mrs. Wakefield and Steven were sitting in the middle of the third row.

"Thanks again," Todd whispered.

Amy gave him a smile. "Break a leg and don't be nervous." Todd nodded, then took a few deep breaths before he took his place around the curtain.

Lloyd Benson and Maria began to hoist some ropes, and the main curtain began to lift. The audience clapped as Janet Howell, the narrator, stepped onto the stage.

"*Two households, both alike in dignity, / In fair*

Verona, where we lay our scene . . ." Janet's grand voice rang out as she began to recite the prologue.

Where's Elizabeth, anyway? Amy wondered. She tried to calm down. It would be several minutes before it was time for Juliet to make her entrance.

In the wings, on the other side of the stage, Amy saw Dennis Cookman in his nurse costume begin to mince and prance around.

Amy craned her neck. Behind Alex and Jake, who were playing Capulet and Montague servants, she caught a glimpse of Juliet. *Hmmm, that's weird,* she thought. Because Juliet's first entrance was from stage right, where Amy stood.

Elizabeth stood several feet behind Amy, anxiously watching the brief conversation between Juliet's mother and Juliet's nurse.

"I bade her come," Dennis Cookman said, twitching the fabric of his skirts. *"Where's this girl? What, Juliet!"*

Elizabeth's heart fluttered as she heard her cue. She started forward and then stopped in a dramatic pause. She closed her eyes and took a deep breath, preparing herself for her big entrance.

Elizabeth lifted her head and lowered her shoulders. She started forward, then jerked to a stop as the sound of crashing applause filled the auditorium.

Juliet had just made her entrance.

From stage left!

Elizabeth began trembling with rage as Jessica paused onstage, simpered slightly in the direction of the audience to acknowledge their applause, and then began to deliver her lines.

Elizabeth ground her teeth. No more dramatic pauses for her. She wasn't going to give Jessica another opportunity to beat her onto the stage.

Todd turned his back toward stage right and extended his hand toward stage left, where Juliet was due to enter for the scene of Romeo and Juliet's meeting.

"My lips, two blushing pilgrims, ready stand." Todd's voice quavered as he unsuccessfully tried to smother a yawn. *"Toooomoothaaaat."*

How weird, Jessica thought. *I've heard of people getting the hiccups when they're nervous, but I've never heard of anyone getting the yawns.*

Todd blinked hard. *". . . rough tough with a tender . . . a tender . . . a tender . . ."* His lips parted for another wide yawn. *". . . a tender kiss,"* he finished.

Jessica knew there wasn't a moment to lose. She lurched forward from stage right just as Todd was finishing his line. "GOOD PILGRIM YOU DO WRONG YOUR HAND TOO MUCH!" Jessica bellowed just in case Elizabeth had any ideas about speaking over her.

Todd jumped when her voice boomed behind him—and he whirled around so fast, he tripped over his feet and fell heavily to the floor. Jessica ignored the giggles and guffaws from the audience.

She acted her scene perfectly, once she got used to Romeo yawning in her face every few minutes.

As Jessica hurried into the wings, she couldn't help giving Amy and Maria a smug smile as they rolled the balcony set toward the stage in preparation for the big balcony scene. *The cold medicine should be kicking in right about now,* she thought triumphantly. *Which means the surplus Juliet is probably sleeping way too soundly to cause any more problems.*

She gazed excitedly at the balcony set, which was now standing on the other side of the stage. Soon she would be up there, performing one of the most beautiful, romantic scenes of all time. She smoothed the front of her dress, took a deep breath, and . . . let out a startled gasp.

Someone had popped up out of the balcony like a rabbit out of a top hat.

Someone who looked exactly like her, wearing *her* costume.

Elizabeth's heart was pounding. This was it. Her big moment. The most famous line in all of Shakespeare's works, and she, Elizabeth Wakefield, was going to deliver it on the stage of Sweet Valley Middle School to her very own Romeo—Todd Wilkins.

There was an expectant hush in the audience.

Elizabeth took a deep breath and gazed soulfully toward the sky. "O *Romeo, Romeo! wherefore art thoooooowwwwYEOW!*" she shrieked as a hand reached up from nowhere, grabbed the back of her hair, and yanked with all its might.

Amy frowned as Elizabeth disappeared from view, ducking down under the balcony wall like a puppet. What in the world was she up to? This wasn't the way the scene had been rehearsed.

Juliet popped up again. She reached her arms out as if in entreaty. "*Deny thy father and refuse thy naaa— HEY!*" Juliet broke off and disappeared once more.

Seconds later, she popped up again, her hair an unruly mess and her cap askew. "*Or if thou wilt not* . . . let go! . . . *Or if thou wilt not* . . . LET GO OF ME! . . . *be but sworn my love.*"

Juliet disappeared from view again. "*And I'll no longer be a Capulet,*" came the muffled line from inside the bucket of the balcony.

The audience began to rustle and whisper as a scuffling sound came from somewhere within the balcony set, punctuated by a few grunts and "oomphs."

"Go on," Mr. Bowman hissed to Todd, who hovered uncertainly in the wings.

"Stop it!" came a voice from inside the balcony.

"You stop it," said a second voice.

Todd yawned and then gingerly approached the

balcony. He paused beside it, while the piece of scenery began to vibrate and sway. *"Shall I hear more, or shall I speak at this?"*

The audience roared with laughter.

Amy bit her lip. *Romeo and Juliet* wasn't exactly supposed to be a comedy. She didn't know where the extra Juliet had come from, but she had a feeling that becoming involved in the whole crazy mess had been a mistake.

Sixteen

Elizabeth hid herself in the fold of the curtain, impatiently waiting for Jessica to make her brief exit so that the real Juliet could reenter in her place. Elizabeth had gotten so flustered by the balcony scene that Jessica had beaten her to the orchard scene.

Elizabeth wrung her hands. Todd was taking forever to get his lines out, probably because he was yawning so much.

Some Romeo he's turning out to be, she thought. *How romantic is it to yawn in your leading lady's face?*

"*Juliet? Juliet?*" she heard Dennis Cookman call from the wings on the opposite side of the stage.

"*Yes, Nurse. I'm coming,*" Jessica cried, exiting toward Dennis.

"*Farewell, farewell! One kiss, and I'll descend,*" Todd called after her.

Elizabeth unrolled herself out of the curtain so fast that the momentum sent her twirling onto the stage.

Todd turned as she twirled toward him.

"OMMMPHHH!" they both cried at exactly the same time as they collided into each other face first.

Again, the audience roared with laughter.

"What a kiss!" a boy called from the audience.

This time the audience began to applaud as Todd stumbled offstage.

Elizabeth stood firmly onstage. There would be no more stumbling from her. She delivered her last lines as passionately and dramatically as possible under the circumstances.

"Whoever you are," Amy whispered to Elizabeth as she left the stage to thundering applause, "you'd better run. You've got trouble coming."

Elizabeth turned and her eyes widened with fear. Mr. Bowman was glaring at her.

"What's going on?" he demanded as he bore down upon her. "And who are you?"

Elizabeth bit her lip for a moment. What was it that Jessica had said about the stage? *There are no such things as friends in the theater, darling.* She took a deep breath. She was going to have to take her sister's words to heart. "Oh, Mr. Bowman," she said in a teary voice, "Elizabeth is just ruining everything."

*   *   *

Jessica sped toward the folding table that held powder, brushes, and lipstick. She had ten minutes before her big death scene.

Suddenly, a hand closed over the back of her dress. "Hold it right there, Elizabeth Wakefield," a familiar voice ordered.

Jessica managed to crane her neck and see Mr. Bowman glaring down at her.

"I'm surprised at you, Elizabeth."

"Elizabeth!" Jessica squeaked in protest. "I'm not . . ."

Mr. Bowman let go of her dress and took her arm, propelling her forward toward the dressing room. "I want you to go in the dressing room and stay there—do you understand? You've created quite enough confusion for one night."

"But Mr. Bowman," Jessica began again.

"I forbid you to leave this room in that costume," Mr. Bowman said. "If you do, then I will give you an F for the entire semester. Is that clear?"

"But . . ."

"Is that clear?"

"Yes, sir," Jessica said in a small voice.

Elizabeth lay perfectly still on the pallet that was supposed to be her burial place.

It was the death scene. The scene in which Romeo arrived at Juliet's tomb with his servant. Romeo would mistakenly believe that she was dead. And after a long, distraught speech, he would drink some poison and die. Only when he hit the floor would Juliet awaken from her slumber.

She felt Todd touch her hand and begin his speech. *"Let me peruse this face . . ."* he said in a thick, sleepy voice. He let out a long, loud, gasping yawn and slithered to the floor with a soft thump.

Elizabeth lay there for a moment, confused. What was Todd doing on the floor? He had lots more lines to deliver before he fell down dead. Maybe he was drawing out the pause for dramatic effect.

She waited.

And waited.

And waited.

There was a confused murmur from the audience.

As subtly as possible, Elizabeth opened her eyes and looked at Todd. He was slumped in a heap on the floor as if he were dead. Maybe all the confusion had made him so mixed up, he forgot his lines. "Todd," she whispered.

There was no answer. "Todd!" she whispered a little louder. "You're not dead yet."

"ZZzzzzzz," came a gentle snore.

The front row of the audience began to snicker, and Elizabeth felt a sense of cold dread stealing over her. She was supposed to be in a deathlike sleep, so she couldn't exactly sit up and shake Romeo awake. In fact, she couldn't move at all. She was stuck lying in a deathlike sleep with her Romeo snoring on the floor.

The dressing room door burst open, and Jessica jumped to her feet.

"Whoever you are, you've got to do something," Amy said in a breathless, panicky voice.

"What are you talking about?" Jessica demanded. "What's wrong?"

"It's Todd—I think he must have taken too much cold medicine or something. It's like he's drugged."

Jessica shook her head. "No, no. You're getting the story confused. Juliet is drugged, but Romeo is poisoned."

"Well, whatever Romeo is, he's out cold. Sound asleep onstage while Juliet lies there locked in a deathlike slumber." She shook her head. "I can't figure out how somebody could fall asleep after gulping down a cold soda. It seems like the caffeine would keep him awake."

Jessica gasped. *Cold soda?* Suddenly this play was starting to make a lot more sense.

"What's the matter?"

"He is drugged," Jessica said gloomily. "But what do you expect me to do about it?"

Amy pawed through the costume trunk and threw Jessica a pair of black-and-gold tights and a red doublet. "Whether you're Jessica or Elizabeth, you know the whole play backwards and forwards.

Tie your hair back in a ponytail and go on for Todd."

Jessica dropped the tights and the doublet. "Let her lie there in a deathlike slumber all night."

"Please, Jessica," Amy pleaded. "You've got to help."

"After what she's done to me? Ha! Give me one good reason why I should help her."

Amy looked at her urgently. "Well, if you're Elizabeth, you'll do it because it's the nice thing to do and it's for the good of the play and you always come through for Jessica. And if you're Jessica, you'll do it because you're genetically incapable of passing up a chance to star in a leading role."

"Give them a three-second blackout," Amy instructed breathlessly as she ran to the light board.

Lloyd Benson shrugged. "Sure, whatever. Nothing else in this crazy production is making any sense." He put his hand on a switch and the stage lights went black.

"One . . . two . . . three . . ." Amy whispered. "OK, let's light 'em up."

Lloyd flipped the switch again.

Romeo lay sprawled next to Juliet's pallet, then he slowly rose. *"How oft when men are at the point of death / Have they been merry! which their keepers call / A lightening before death."*

Romeo leaned over Juliet's prone body, and his chin sank to his chest in despair. *"O my love! my wife!"*

Romeo's voice broke on a note of pure anguish. A chill ran up Amy's spine.

"Death that hath sucked the honey of thy breath / Hath had no power yet upon thy beauty."

Tears sprang to Amy's eyes as the scene went on. Lloyd Benson and the other crew members stood perfectly still, with their attention riveted on the stage. The terrible tragedy of *Romeo and Juliet* was coming to life in a way that had never happened in the course of the rehearsals.

Romeo lifted the vial of poison to his lips. Amy wrung her hands.

"O true apothecary! / Thy drugs are quick. Thus with a kiss I die." Romeo tossed the poison down and then fell to the floor.

Moments later, Juliet slowly awakened from her drugged sleep. *"Where is my Romeo?"* she asked. *"What's here? / A cup, closed in my true love's hand? / Poison, I see, hath been his timeless end."*

Amy's arms broke out in goose bumps. Juliet's surprise and heartbreak were so sad and so tragic.

Juliet lifted her dagger, stabbed herself, and fell beside Romeo.

As the stage lights began to lower, Amy heard sobs from the audience. Then, after a long, stunned pause, the audience erupted in thunderous applause. "BRAVO! BRAVO!"

Romeo and Juliet both climbed gracefully to

their feet, gave each other a broad grin, then joined hands and bowed low.

Amy looked out at the audience. The parents, teachers, and students were giving Romeo and Juliet a standing ovation.

"Bravo! Bravo!"

Amy looked across the stage to see who that particularly loud cheer was coming from. It was Mr. Bowman. And on his cheek, Amy saw the distinct glitter of a tear.

"Ughh!" Amy said on Monday morning after second period as Jessica and Elizabeth came walking toward her. "You two look gross! What's with the warts?"

Jessica lifted her notebook to try to shield her warty cheek from view.

Elizabeth laughed and patted the large wart on the end of her nose. "Mr. Bowman said that in spite of the great job we did at the end of the show, he couldn't overlook all the stuff we did at the beginning. So he gave us a choice. We could each take an *F* for the week . . ."

"Which I can't afford to do," Jessica groaned. "My grade point average is shaky as it is."

". . . or, we could spend the day in face warts," Elizabeth finished.

"Well, I'll say this for Mr. Bowman," Amy said, laughing, "he's definitely got a sense of humor."

"A sick sense of humor," Jessica said sourly,

lifting her notebook again as Rick Hunter and Bruce Patman gave a double take as they passed the twins.

"Hey, look on the bright side, Jess," Elizabeth said. "You're getting a lot of attention from cute guys."

"Believe me," Jessica replied, "I'd rather get attention as a tragic romantic heroine." Her eyes sparkled as she looked at Elizabeth over her notebook. "Or at least a tragic romantic *hero*."

"So did your folks punish you?" Amy asked Elizabeth at lunch.

Elizabeth shrugged. "They just gave us a long lecture," she answered. "Actually, it was *me* that got the long lecture. Jessica got off pretty much scot-free if you don't count the warts."

"How come you got a long lecture and Jessica didn't?" Amy asked.

Elizabeth shrugged. "Oh, you know. They sort of went on and on about how I'm more mature than most kids my age and they would have expected better behavior from me."

"Well, I guess that's pretty logical," Amy commented. "You're so responsible and hardworking and all that. Everybody always expects a lot from you."

Elizabeth's face darkened a little. "I know," she said unhappily. "But sometimes . . ." She trailed off and didn't finish her sentence.

Amy waited a few moments. "Sometimes what?" she asked softly.

Elizabeth sighed. "Sometimes I feel like they expect too much," she answered in a quiet voice. "Sometimes I feel like I just can't measure up."

Can Elizabeth meet everyone's high expectations? Find out in Sweet Valley Twins #85, **Elizabeth the Seventh-Grader.**

Bantam Books in the SWEET VALLEY TWINS series.
Ask your bookseller for the books you have missed.

Sweet Valley Twins Super Editions

Sweet Valley Twins Super Chiller Editions

Sweet Valley Twins Magna Editions

SIGN UP FOR THE SWEET VALLEY HIGH® FAN CLUB!

Hey, girls! Get all the gossip on Sweet Valley High's® most popular teenagers when you join our fantastic Fan Club! As a member, you'll get all of this really cool stuff:

- Membership Card with your own personal Fan Club ID number
- A Sweet Valley High® Secret Treasure Box
- Sweet Valley High® Stationery
- Official Fan Club Pencil (for secret note writing!)
- Three Bookmarks
- A "Members Only" Door Hanger
- Two Skeins of J. & P. Coats® Embroidery Floss with flower barrette instruction leaflet
- Two editions of *The Oracle* newsletter
- Plus exclusive Sweet Valley High® product offers, special savings, contests, and much more!

Be the first to find out what Jessica & Elizabeth Wakefield are up to by joining the Sweet Valley High® Fan Club for the one-year membership fee of only $6.25 each for U.S. residents, $8.25 for Canadian residents (U.S. currency). Includes shipping & handling.

Send a check or money order (do not send cash) made payable to "Sweet Valley High® Fan Club" along with this form to:

SWEET VALLEY HIGH® FAN CLUB, BOX 3919-B, SCHAUMBURG, IL 60168-3919

NAME _____
(Please print clearly)

ADDRESS _____

CITY_____ STATE _____ ZIP_____
(Required)

AGE _____ BIRTHDAY_____ /_____ /_____

Offer good while supplies last. Allow 6-8 weeks after check clearance for delivery. Addresses without ZIP codes cannot be honored. Offer good in USA & Canada only. Void where prohibited by law.
©1993 by Francine Pascal   LCI-1383-123